POLAR SWAP

POLAR SWAP

by
Arthur Herzog

iUniverse, Inc.
New York   Bloomington

Polar Swap

iUniverse books may be ordered through booksellers or by contacting:

iUniverse
1663 Liberty Drive
Bloomington, IN 47403
www.iuniverse.com
1-800-Authors (1-800-288-4677)

ISBN: 978-1-4401-0828-0 (pbk)
ISBN: 978-1-4401-0829-7 (ebk)

Printed in the United States of America

iUniverse rev. date: 12/17/2008

By the same author:

FICTION

The Third State
Body Parts
The Town That Moved to Mexico
The Village Buyers
Imortalon
Icetopia
Beyond Sci-Fi
L*S*I*T*T (in softcover: Takeover)
The Craving
Aries Rising
Glad to be Here
Make Us Happy
IQ 83
Orca
Heat
Earthsound
The Swarm

NONFICTION

A Murder in Our Town
How to Write Almost Anything Better and Faster
Seventeen Days: The Katie Beers Story
The Woodchipper Murder
Vesco: From Wall Street to Castro's Cuba
The B.S. Factor
McCarthy for President
The Church Trap
The War/Peace Establishment
Smoking in the Public Interest

For
Bob Brooks

ACKNOWLEDGEMENTS

Dr. Alexander J. Dessler, Rice University; Dr. Dennis Kent, Dr. Walter Pitman and Dr. James Hayes, Lamont-Doherty Geological Observatory; Dr. Steve Hahn; Dr. Carol Raymond, Jet Propulsion Laboratory, Pasadena, California; Dr. Rene Eastin, Southampton College; Dr. Joseph L. Kirschvink, California Institute of Technology and Dr. Mark Morell and Michael Novacek of the American Museum of Natural History. Dr. Robert Brooks; Joseph H. Spigelman, *Toward a New Foundation for Physics*, Dr. Jeff Buss, and Dr. Rafal Jakubowski, Dr. Piotr Chabecki and Magdalena Droszcz.

For several years, scientists studying Earth through spacecraft observations have noted...a steady decline in the intensity of the magnetic field. They postulate this could be the early sign of an approaching magnetic reversal.

Earth's magnetic poles should do a flip-flop, and all those compass needles that normally point north will then be pointing south.

-The New York Times, June 17, 1980

A polar reversal would first disrupt, then ultimately reverse, the orientation of all compasses, affecting every guidance system, including those in missiles, spacecraft, aircraft and ships. Evolution would also be quickly affected.

Most significantly, a reversal could indirectly cause major climate changes.

- University of Minnesota Conference Report, 1983

Throughout most, if not all, of the earth's history, its magnetic field has reversed itself at irregular intervals of thousands of years.

While the magnetism is believed to be generated by motions of the earth's liquid core, the reason for reversals is mysterious.

- The New York Times, June 18, 1991

Scientists aren't sure what results a polar swap might be except for one - - the greatest disaster mankind has ever known.

- Journal of Science, February 10, 2002

Everything contains the seeds of its own opposite.

Asian saying

PART ONE

Chapter One

A NIGHTMARE?

Yes, it was him inside a large room beneath old rafters. Mortal danger lurked above. In the flickering light he could barely see the computer screen where Magsat reported a magnetic storm as the North and South Poles were about to fuse with perhaps the disastrous results Darius had predicted when almost no one would listen. He'd been accused of a neurotic fixation on the distant past and the limits of human knowledge but didn't feel good about having been right. Darius heard a baby cry and he verged on tears. Should he abandon hope? No, but - -

#

Even in northern Canada, it sweltered.

She wiped the sweat off her breasts, stretched, and looked outside through the casement window at the bleak landscape. Nothing moved except goats.

The snow had long since melted but the fields were parched. No rain for weeks, they'd told her. It hadn't been called a drought but soon would, she figured.

The weather explained why she was in Canada instead of Chicago, her home. Dahlia missed the windy city and yearned to return as soon as possible.

She wouldn't be alone here, thank God. The furnished farmhouse she had just bought on e-Bay had too many rooms for a single person so she'd advertised on Cyberentals. Dahlia needed companionship, not cash.

An obvious target was people from California. The torrid sun blazed there. She'd seen on TV that, according to the National Institutes of Health and Prevention, skin cancer and blindness had reached pandemic levels in Los Angeles.

Dahlia also knew from TV some scientists blamed the lingering effect of the ozone hole's depletion. Other scientists argued that couldn't be the cause but seemed vague about the real answer. Still, the equatorial zone now extended from mid-Mexico to Argentina. Similar situations had occurred throughout the world though few but climatologists admitted it despite the arrival of parrots in temperate regions and squawked noisily. Ordinary people believed they'd escaped from cages.

To avoid the constant threat of melanoma and wrecked retinas individuals used extra-strength sunblock and wore dark glasses plus long-sleeved protective gear in spite of the record heat. The fashion industry had given up the effort to make women's clothes attractive.

Dahlia, like many Americans, had moved to Canada. She'd chosen the village, Resolute, because the name matched her spirit, she felt.

Flooded with Cyberental applicants, she'd picked those who seemed unique, as interesting as her, and more or less in the same age bracket.

Darius Sykes - - 33 years old, (he e-mailed) associate professor of paleomagnetism at Caltech in Pasadena, CA.

She e-mailed him. "What does paleo mean?"

"Incredibly ancient," he immediately responded.

"How ancient?"

"Pre-Jurassic."

When a teenager Dahlia had been thrilled by the film "Jurassic Park" which she watched several times with her buddies. "Are you a dinosaur expert?"

"Not in the conventional sense."

A puzzling reply. Intrigued, she had one more question.

"Married?"

"Negative."

"No, that is?'

"Affirmative."

This exchange settled the matter and consumed fifteen minutes. She invited the paleomagnetist to head north, suggesting Air Alaska as the best to reach Nome. Regarding the rest, she'd be in contact. Dahlia patted her Chihuahua.

The second chosen person, Wendy Goto, who by e-mail said that she was a neurosurgeon and psychiatrist affiliated with UCal/Berkeley near San Francisco. 33 years young, Japanese-American. Used to be a ballet dancer. Requires a lot of exercise and now works out in a swimming pool. Read all kinds of books.

Fine. Shelves of dusty books had come with the house but Dahlia wasn't much of a reader. She preferred TV. Always had.

Split from my lover and don't intend to reconcile.

Hmmm. Was the woman trustworthy?

Have a small number of friends, none close. On an extended l.o.a. (leave of absence) - -

Condescending bitch! I know what l.o.a. stands for.

- - can travel at once.

Dahlia, pondering, delayed an answer, but finally gave an o.k. She contemplated the next, Walter Gertz, a full professor - -

What separated associate and full? Could the two bridge the gap?

- - of electrical engineering at MIT. Enjoying a sabbatical. Thirty-nine years old, Gertz had recently endured a nasty divorce and his ex-wife had taken him to the proverbial cleaners even though they lacked kids. He was finished with women period. He lifted weights instead.

He seemed like a man not to trifle with and Dahlia grinned. She admired the man's honesty and strength; and he wasn't just a person who wanted to escape California's intense heat and blindness. Dahlia decided probably to accept him.

Walter continued: he had various hobbies and was a former officer in the Air Force Reserve. Nothing frightened him, he asserted.

Which sounded good, Dahlia thought.

If I risked the future on Goto, I'll do it again with Gertz.

In a rapid series of e-mails, Dahlia told her new tenants to proceed to Nome via Air Alaska…charged to her credit card…and ask for Gus, a pilot Dahlia had met when she flew to Resolute. She phoned him and heard static on the line. Why? Dahlia wondered. Finally, Gus understood. He'd be expecting the group. He found them because Dahlia had given Gus their names.

#

On the side, Gus flew an oil company jet, a Gulfstream IV. As instructed by Dahlia the passengers toted scant luggage. Aboard the plane, Walter asked what the destination was.

"Ain't Shangri-la," Gus said.

"Shangri-la?" Darius jumped up. "A venereal disease?"

Wendy remarked in a low throbbing voice, batting her dark eyelashes, "A Buddhist paradise high in the Himalayas where you never grow old unless you leave. A utopia that can become a dystopia."

"Huh?" Walter mouthed.

"A bad utopia also called a kakatopia which means shit."

"Does Shangri-la exist?" Walter asked.

"No. It's a novel <u>Lost</u> <u>Horizo</u>n, by James Hilton. Read fiction?"

"Only scientific stuff." Darius said. "You?"

"Every book I can put my hands on."

"Close to the Bering Sea," Gus was telling Walter. All of them sat in the pilot's cabin, thanks to Gus. The view could only be described as magnificent - - wispy clouds against a crystalline sky. You could see the curvature of the earth and Darius reflected on human knowledge, slow to accumulate. Even as the masts of tall ships gradually disappeared over the horizon, people went on believing the world was flat instead of round. Common sense. Millennia passed before they accepted the shocking truth which then seemed illogical. What lay ahead? It gave him a shuddery feeling.

The universe contained trillions of stars, many with planets. Who could grasp what was happening out there?

The gods, then one god in our culture, provided a rational explanation. But science supplanted gods. Soon, atheism, the logical next step, would prevail. Could atheistic scientists like him fare better? Though hoping so he had doubts.

Crossing the snow-capped mountains, Gus reported instrument problems. "I'm uncertain which way is north."

Darius cast a worried gaze, biting his lower lip. "Might a change in terrestrial - -"

"Terrestrial?"

"Earthly."

"Oh. Well, perhaps. But I've flown this route many times and I can find Resolute." His yellow-toothed smile was full of confidence.

Quickly they glimpsed the grey forbidding ocean. The village appeared beneath with brightly-painted fishing boats, a tavern and a general store. Each carried neon signs.

"The airstrip is long, built to accommodate jets," the pilot told them. "The road to it reaches the village."

The Gulfstream landed smoothly and a woman met them. She had carrot-colored hair and cinnabar freckles. She carried a dog. "Hello. I'm Dahlia Stanton."

"Doesn't Dahlia mean moonflower?" the other woman asked. Dahlia's face was blank and she, short and big-breasted with Asian eyes, clad in a miniskirt, said, "I'm Wendy." She looked up at the men.

"I'm Gertz," Walter said in a loud bass voice. He was at least 6'2", and solidly constructed. He had black hair and a handsome face. He wore a sleek business suit. He resembled Dick Tracy.

"My name is Darius," said the medium-size blond man in a t-shirt. He had scrawny arms, a concave stomach and a thin frame.

"Glad to meet all of you," Dahlia gushed and stared as if to take their measure. "I own an old Humvee, military surplus; it came with the house. Pile in."

The Chihuahua on her lap, she patted the seat next to her and motioned toward Gertz. Goto and Sykes sat behind them. The vehicle rolled down the bumpy road.

Before much time had elapsed, they saw the town covered in mist that had suddenly formed. "It has a freaking Eskimo name which translates as Resolute because life here is almost unbearably harsh. Only the toughest folks could survive." Dahlia gestured at the gaudy fishing boats and the tavern. "Don't get in trouble here. We're in Canada. We lack U.S. protection." And then the general store. "We don't need much this far north."

"Is that right?" Wendy muttered.

"But you may buy what you need when you're ready."

Dahlia drove on. "No snow," Walter noted.

"It's June. The snow has melted." She paused. "Enjoy the view?"

He gazed at the barren hills. "How many acres did you buy?"

"About ten," Dahlia said.

"Plan on growing crops?" Darius asked.

"I hate hard work."

The Humvee stopped before a house. "Isn't that Gothic style?" Wendy wondered, pointing at the dark exterior, the porches on both floors, the narrow windows, the numerous chimneys covered with ivy.

"Must have cost a bundle," Walter ventured.

"Doesn't matter."

"You're loaded?"

"We'll discuss it during dinner."

They entered the house. "I don't mess with locks," Dahlia said. "There's not much to steal except booze and the Eskimos aren't thieves."

"Sure?" Walter said.

"You're the suspicious type?"

"Blame the divorce lawyers."

"You can't forget?"

"Never," Walter said.

The livingroom had stained-glass windows, massive wooden upholstered furniture, logs neatly stacked around a maw of a fireplace, shelves filled with books.

"Walter will sleep downstairs," Dahlia directed. "Wendy and Darius upstairs. In separate rooms, of course." She arched her russet eyebrows.

"Isn't' that a bit priggish?" Wendy said.

"Where is my bedroom? Walter demanded.

"Near mine." Dahlia aimed a finger.

Darius carried a rucksack, Walter a large suitcase, Wendy a shopping bag.

"You have fifteen minutes to use the bathroom and then we'll assemble for cocktails."

"How would you describe them?" Darius said to Wendy as they climbed the stairs.

"As a psychologist I'd call Dahlia a prude in a libertine's body. She has a juvenile streak. I bet in high school she was a cheerleader."

"Oh. Walter?"

"Passive-aggressive. I bet he's an alcoholic."

"And us?"

"We'll see. How'd you know so much about magnetism?"

"From studying." Darius answered.

"Hard?"

"You can be certain," His eyes had a stubborn quality.

Darius descended the stairs in the same outfit he'd sported on the plane - - a t-shirt with Caltech printed in front, chinos and loafers. Wendy was still attired in a miniskirt, plus platform shoes and brass earrings. Walter had changed clothes. He now wore short pants that revealed his hairy, muscular legs. The grandfather clock in the corner chimed exactly five p.m. "Drink time," Dahlia said.

She waited in a tight-fitting orange dress and low heels. Braless, her breasts showed as she bent to fill the ice bucket. Bottles of every description lined the long table. "I brought the stuff from Chicago. Help yourselves."

Walter strode up and poured a slug of bourbon. He raised the shot glass. "No skin cancer here!"

"Amen," Wendy rejoiced.

"A-women" Dahlia jested.

Darius regarded her solemnly. "Skin cancer isn't a joke."

"To what do you attribute it?" Wendy inquired.

"I can't accept the ozone hole theory. Must be something else."

"For example?"

"The rest of us need drinks first," Dahlia said and poured single malt whiskey into her glass. Wendy chose sake, Darius soda pop.

He remarked, "Where was I? Yes, the ozone hole. I blame magnetism."

"Why?" Wendy murmured.

Chapter Two

Instead of answering, Darius imagined Pasadena ringed with bulldozers that spewed smoke as they dug underground shelters, crews of hardhats laying ramps and bringing supplies, cops forcing the population into them. As best he could he verbalized the scene.

Wendy gasped. "Turning people into troglodytes is unacceptable. The cause?"

Darius hesitated. "In my opinion, a geomagnetic reversal."

Dahlia swilled Scotch. "Speak English."

"A polar swap when the earth's magnetic poles trade places. The compass needle dips south as north becomes south and vice-versa."

"Has this occurred before?"

"Based on measurements of the earth's magnetic field taken since about eighteen hundred fifty some paleomagnetists estimate that the dipoles - -"

"Dipoles?"

"Other, smaller poles. The dipole moment will decay in about thirteen hundred years. However, the present dipole moment is actually higher than it has been for most of the last fifty thousand years and the poles could reverse at any time. If they do, radio and telephone communication would deteriorate, navigation by magnetic compass would be almost impossible and migratory animals would experience difficulties."

"Oh."

He stared at her sullenly and went on, "During the past hundred million years, the reversal rates have varied considerably. Recent rock records indicate reversals happen on time scales of about two hundred thousand years. The last magnetic field reversal was around seven-hundred eighty thousand years back."

Wendy counted on her fingers. "I'm mathematically adroit." she announced. "Averaging every two hundred fifty thousand years. If so, a polar flip-flop is five hundred thousand years late."

"I figure we're due for another."

"How are you cognizant a polar swap happened at all?" Dahlia questioned.

"I'm paleomagnetist, remember? Volcanic activity leaves a record of spectacular magnetic reversals over millennia. They also indicate changes in polarity and striations or stripes, little fault lines. The magnetic field reverses too," he stated. "We know this from fossil rocks and deep sea sediments. An additional important indicator is that the level of terrestrial magnetism has been sinking for at least three hundred years."

"It has?" the engineer said skeptically, blowing smoke from his cigarette.

"Measurements prove the decline. What bothers me is where the reversal would happen. If through the center of the earth - -"

"Molten rock," he asserted.

"Wrong! Solid iron, the size of the moon - -"

"Reminds me of me," Dahlia cooed.

"Sounds like she's in love with herself. A narcissist," Wendy diagnosed.

Dahlia ignored her. "Moonflower."

"- - which rotates. It seems to be speeding up. A third indicator," Darius droned. "Where was I?"

"Again?" Wendy cried. "Through the center of the earth."

"Correct. Over a period of decades. We might have time to adjust but if - -"

"If?" Dahlia yelped.

"- - the reversal happens on the surface in a day or two - -"

"If?" Dahlia repeated, sounding resigned.

"Bullshit!" Walter raged. "I disagree with Darius." He stamped out the cigarette.

But he refused to provide a reason. Darius suspected competition for the females. Primitive.

"Dahlia served more drinks and looked at the clock. "Let's catch the six o'clock news from California." Using the remote, she clicked on the TV.

Dozens of images flashed in quick succession. Long lines of people with marred facial skin, including a few whose cheeks had been eaten away until teeth showed; they obviously suffered from melanoma and stood in front of a medical clinic. Some, blind as well, clutched the leashes of seeing-eye dogs.

Announcer: "We are losing hope. There is no escape. Alaska lacks housing. Canada barred us today. Barred us today."

"Why is he repeating himself?"

"I don't know. Let's watch," Darius said.

More gruesome images of skin cancer victims.

Dahlia moaned. "Before I lose my appetite, let's have dinner."

Click.

Dahlia in the lead, they moved to the kitchen, a large, raftered room. Pots and pans hung over a stainless steel sink near a polished pine table. Heat came from a cast-iron stove. In it, something cooked.

Evidently smelling the aroma, Walter salivated. Runnels appeared on his wide mouth.

"What's for dinner?"

"Bouillabaisse. I bought the fish from the Eskimos but they lacked rascasse."

"Cuss a ras? Black folks' slang?" Darius seemed awkwardly amused.

"French for stonefish, an essential ingredient."

"Where'd you learn that?" Wendy wondered.

"Hortense, a French chef, who cooked for my parents."

"Did they have guests?"

"Banquets in the dining hall for the country club crowd."

"Rich?"

"All of them. And dead."

"Too bad."

"Time to feed the dog. Where is she?" Dahlia whistled but nothing happened.

"Where is it?" Darius said.

"Must have got lost in this big house," Walter said.

"No. Come, Taca."

"Taca?" Wendy asked.

"A female Mexican dog which loves to eat. Taca - -"

"There," Darius pointed at a tail in the corner, "It could be dead."

Dahlia's eyes filled with tears as she inspected the dog. "Right. But how?"

"Put the hound in the freezer," Wendy remarked. "I'll perform an autopsy soon. You were saying?"

"The country club crowd."

"Dead? Moribund?"

"They all died young. A fate I hope to avoid."

"By staying childish?"

"I remember my girlhood. Mother put me in beauty contests but I refused to attend. I'd rip up my dress and demand a new one."

"Did you win?"

Dahlia nodded.

"Your age then?"

"Five or six."

"Go on competing?"

"In high school I twirled a baton and became a cheerleader."

"I <u>knew</u> it. How did your parents die?"

"Killed in a car crash."

"You mother worked?"

Dahlia frowned, "Being a socialite is work."

"Your father's occupation?"

"The relevance?"

"I'll be the judge of that."

"O.K. CEO of a railroad, based in Chicago."

"That's why giving orders seems natural to you?"

"I suppose. Dad had a private railroad car. We traveled everywhere."

"Spoiled?"

"For sure." She again frowned.

"Brothers and/or sisters?"

"I was the only child."

"Lonely?"

"But I stood on my own two feet."

"An independent type. Always like that?"

"So many questions, Goto."

"To hell with me, you mean."

"I suspect you're being cursive. Inherit their dough?"

"Uh-huh."

Walter smiled encouragingly. "Tell us still more about you."

"Such as how much bread? Maybe millions. I won't say. Your turn. Be honest if you can."

"Concerning? I informed you I was on a sabbatical…a paid year off for every seven worked…which wasn't quite accurate. I was forced to take an extended vacation - -"

"A permanent vacation?"

Walter ignored her. "-- because of unimportant liaisons with other women. The facts emerged during my divorce."

"How did you meet them?"

"Playing bridge at the Jewish country club."

"Are you Jewish?"

"Half Jewish. I call myself a semi-Semite. My brother and I joked that together we're a whole Yid." He laughed hollowly.

"What happened to him?"

"Committed suicide."

"Why?"

"I'd rather not divulge that information."

"O.K."

"Which parent was Jewish?" Wendy asked.

"My father."

"His job?"

"A butcher. He loved meat."

"Fat?"

"Three hundred pounds."

"Were you a chubby kid?"

"Yeah, but I exercised and lost weight. I'm proud of it, just as I'm proud of my card skills. I'm a champion. Broads for me have always been, in the parlance of bridge, laydowns."

"A womanizer!" Dahlia shrieked.

"Semi," Walter said smoothly.

"And a schizo, I bet," Wendy whispered. Walter ignored her and Dahlia didn't seem to hear. "Who else has lied to me?" she shouted.

Wendy raised a timid hand. "I failed to present the unvarnished truth. I said I had a lover but I neglected to specify the gender. She was a nurse at my hospital."

"A lesbian!" Dahlia yelled. "Small wonder you've had few consorts."

"Bi-sexuality was an experiment. I tried it after I had an abortion."

"The father?"

"Don't know. I was raped one night after ballet class. Even so, my parents insisted I continue. They had had great expectations for me."

"Why?"

"They owned a sushi bar and wanted me to run it."

"What happened to them?" Dahlia asked.

"Went bankrupt," she said with sadness.

"Why?"

"I'd prefer not to go into that. Wanted me to excel, and I did."

"When in doubt," Darius advised, "honesty is best."

"O.K.," Wendy said. "I stole money from the sushi bar and my folks were forced out of business. But I was the high school valedictorian. That's about all - -"

"Go on."

"She's shy," Walter said.

Wendy smiled. "I'd hoped to find new friends here and I've rediscovered I adore men." Blushing, she ogled Darius.

He said, gazing back, "I too have a confession. I'm a coward. That applies to women and being proud of myself."

"Sounds like low self-esteem" Wendy said.

"Undoubtedly. When a kid, I had acne and I stuttered."

"Neither now," Wendy said.

"But the low self-regard remained."

"Explain," Dahlia urged, "And give us a for instance."

He inhaled. "All right. My folks "they were teachers" named me after a Persian emperor who defied Alexander the Great. Despite the size of the Persian army he won the largest battle in ancient times. Technology...the phalanx...led to Alexander's triumph, but Darius had shown tremendous grit which is what my dad wanted to instill. But I felt I couldn't compete with <u>that</u> Darius, being rectidudinous."

"Oh dear," Dahlia sympathized.

"However, I stuck to my guns regarding my Ph.D thesis at CalTech titled 'Death of the Dinosaurs'. It was challenged by my professors who considered the premise unlikely so I chose another, duller subject."

"Where were you writing your thesis?"

"I rented a dilapidated house...call it a shack...in Pasadena. It mostly consisted of tables on saw horses, a hard couch and a cot."

"Kitchen?"

Darius laughed. "A hotplate. I ordered Chinese."

"Eat by yourself?"

"Always. I worked."

"Have a pet?"

"Negative. I detest small animals."

"A natural hermit," Wendy diagnosed. "Worked on what?"

"My original notion."

"Which was?"

Darius coughed. "A polar swap rendered them extinct."

"How?"

"They lost their sense of direction, wandered into bogs and drowned. I prepared a simulation."

"We insist on viewing it," Dahlia said, sounding regal.

"Have you a computer in the kitchen?"

"Every room."

"I'll fetch the eight MB jump drive."

Dahlia uncorked bottles of wine from the cellar.

Darius returned and inserted the jump drive into the USB port. The computer sat on a table in the corner. They saw

Thick clouds floated over a dark, volcanic landscape covered by swatches of dense mist. A high wind stirred six feet tall tropical ferns growing beside soupy bodies of water.

A superimposed dial showed the four compass points and a red arrow.

N
W ↑ E
S

The arrow swung east. A break in the clouds revealed a procession of dots streaming south.

A pterodactyl swooped from a jagged cliff, aiming for a pond, flew too near a giant tree whose branches caught a bony wing. Mouth open, the pterodactyl plunged to the ground.

Giant frogs with teeth lurked.

On a grassy plain dinosaurs by the hundreds stood absolutely still, heads raised, as if they'd received a signal.

The arrow continued to turn.

$$N$$
$$W \searrow E$$
$$S$$

As if bewildered, the dinosaurs galloped in every direction, crashing into each other, dropping, being trampled, until countless creatures lay on the plain.

Some attacked each other with claws and teeth.

Others charged blindly into a swamp, sank, disappeared. Huge bolts of lightening pierced torrential rain.

#

The screen faded, leaving a flashing arrow pointed south.

N

W ↓ E

S

"Better than a flick," Wendy whispered.

"Never happened," Walter said brusquely.

"What?"

"The fucking dinosaurs' confusion. Pure guesswork."

"The question ought to be why did it happen," Dahlia said, curling her lips.

Darius yanked an earlobe. "I suspect the dinos - -"

"Dinos?"

"An affectionate abbreviation for the creatures - -"

"Affectionate? You have feelings for the reptiles?" Walter said accusingly.

"Perhaps I identify with them." He laughed. "They had magnetite in their skulls."

"Magnetite?"

"A rare metal that responds to magnetism and found in lodestones which the Chinese used in antiquity for primitive compasses."

"Any bearing on us?"

"We may also have trace magnetite in our craniums."

"The effect?"

"In the midst of a geomagnetic polarity reversal - -"

"Yes, yes," Dahlia said impatiently. "I was wrong. Not why, to me an often unanswerable question - -"

"And it applies to the universe," Darius added. We'll get to that later, I'm certain."

"- - but how would the phenomenon occur?"

"- - inside the iron ball at the earth's center, magnetic eddies form and when the southerly-pointed ones, which have been gaining strength, outnumber the northernly-pointed ones, a polar swap ensues. The compass needle heads south and we lose our sense of direction."

"That's all?"

"Enough to cause a disaster. And....I'm merely speculating...our speech might change."

"How?" Dahlia again asked.

"I suppose we could talk backwards and act the opposite from our normal selves."

"The new normal? Scary."

Darius remembered a magnetic axiom: likes attract, opposites repel.

Conservative Dahlia was indeed attractive to him but he, a leftist, fell silent.

"I'm a San Francisco radical," Wendy announced." A left-wing, Nancy Pelosi (bless her soul) Democrat." From Darius she averted her eyes.

Likes attract, he thought.

Dahlia pondered. "Wouldn't the maps need to be reversed? The east coast located in the west, where we are, and the west in the east?"

"Wait a minute," Wendy said with a mischievous smile. "The same thing must apply to north and south. Japan, my ancestral country, must reside in the southern hemisphere."

"Australia would become Greenland, I suppose. I should purchase stock in a company that makes maps like McNally Rand. Rand McNally I meant to say."

The others stared at her.

Dahlia drank wine. "Is it possible our alcohol intake reverses?"

"Why not?"

Darius said. "I'm a teetotaler. I might climb off the wagon."

"Me too," Wendy chimed. "I might trade sake for dry martinis." She took the dog to the freezer.

"I could, probably should, join AA," Dahlia said. "Walter too."

He thrust forth his glass and failed to utter a word.

"Continue, Darius," Dahlia said.

He sipped soda pop. "Well, left-handed people could become right handed and the other way round."

"Righties turn into lefties? Conservatives radical? Not me," Walter said.

"You're a Republican?" Wendy asked, frowning.

"Dyed in the wool."

"Ditto," Dahlia said. "We'll eat here," and she brought utensils, crockery and napkins. She removed the fish from the oven and served it.

The verdict: "Marvelous."

Dahlia tasted. "Agreed."

Out of nowhere, Darius remarked, "I was contemplating evolution. Does nature conjure up those strange shapes? Like the wingless wasp that eats grasshoppers, the giraffe or hippo...only a few of them survive I've read...or the narwhal's long tusk. Must be defense against killer whales because the creature is otherwise helpless. Still, it's such a clumsy weapon! Nature would have devised something better had it imagination which, of course, it lacks. Nature proceeds by trial and error."

"Why are you telling us this?" Dahlia demanded.

"Because a polar swap might affect evolution. For instance, the dinos devolved into birds. What form would humans take if a post-reversal world proves hostile? We might grow tusks instead of teeth!"

"Unattractive," Dahlia said.

"We'd need a tusk dentist. Or become gentle with no defenses."

"Flim-flammery," Walter shouted.

"You'll find out - -"

TWO

Chapter Three

"ARGUMENTS ARE FORBIDDEN DURING dinner," Dahlia admonished. They finished eating in silence.

The table cleared of dishes, Wendy lifted the Chihuahua from the floor. She stared at it, then with a carving knife, removed a leg which she examined. "I'm not a forensic expert," she said, "but it seems to me the canine's blood has congealed. That is, ceased to circulate."

"Why for God's sake?" Dahlia cried.

"I don't know."

"Could something similar have happened to the dinos?" Darius wondered. "If so, magnetism must be involved." He looked away.

"Too early for bed," Dahlia said. She sipped wine. "Not enough light here. Let's move upstairs."

The others trouped after her to the second floor and then the roof. The night was chilly with clouds. No moon. Darius pointed. "See that?"

"What?"

"Lights on the distant horizon."

"Lost horizon?"

"If only it were fiction," Wendy said. "What are the lights?"

"The Aurora Borealis. Electrically charged particles of solar wind produced by the sun. It forces them to move along the magnetic field lines both at the poles. When the particles encounter the upper atmosphere, they emit colored light, red, blue, green, called the Auroras. But not till August," responded the former Air Force pilot.

"What he saw must have been lightning."

"Yeah? Where's the thunder?"

"Too far away."

"But - -"

Wendy interrupted. "I'm cold. Let's go down."

They did, a wanton gleam in her eyes. On the second floor, Wendy dashed to her room and changed clothes. Minutes later, she emerged in the livingroom wearing almost transparent pajamas instead of a miniskirt.

Leering, Walter said, "You have a dancer's legs."

"Which means?"

"Sexy."

Seeming jealous, Dahlia snapped, "Time for the news."

Images of a shuttered L.A. medical clinic.

Announcer: "This facility...this facility..."

"Why is he repeating himself?" Darius asked. "We'll find out, I guess."

"...has closed, three hours after the usual time because of the crowd of skin cancer victims and blind folks. The situation continues to deteriorate. When will it end? Never, some believe. Have a good night."

Click.

"At least we're safe," was Dahlia's opinion.

"You're smug but for how long?" Wendy asked.

Walter said, "Solar radiation is bound to diminish soon."

"Not in my view," said Darius. "I mentioned magnetism and the van Allen belts." He yawned. "If they change, the days could be longer or shorter. Plants could die."

Wendy said, "I wanted to stay up and hear more from you."

"Mmmm."

A noncommittal response, he knew.

#

Darius woke with an erection in the narrow chamber that contained a wood-burning stove, sparse furniture, lace curtains on the window and pictures of sailboats on the wall.

Wendy's bedroom lay across the hall and he remembered the previous evening - - she'd kissed him on the lips but he'd mouthed "Mmmm" and turned his back, frightened of getting too close and thinking of Dahlia.

The carrot-haired woman has been peering at Walter when he (Darius) departed. What to make of it?

Darius went to the window from which he could see the corpse-gray ocean and the bosom of the harbor, near enough to bicycle there. Perhaps Dahlia would organize an expedition. And he wondered where the Eskimos lived.

He inspected his watch, a $25 Timex. Just seven a.m. The watch could be affected by magnetism. Was the time correct? For the moment, he'd be alone in the world. Darius went downstairs. Quiet as a mouse in his sandals, he prowled the livingroom. Next to the clock Darius discovered grainy photos Dahlia probably hadn't had time to dispose of. The weathered faces of farmers who'd lived here, he supposed. The entire family must have died since, as Dahlia told him, she'd purchased the place from a probate court. Who were the farmers and who had buried them?

Curious, he walked outside. In the backyard he found a number of tombstones with names inscribed.

Across a hedge Darius spotted a beefy man who lugged a spade. This must be the gardener. His square face and oblong eye sockets spoke of Mongolian genes. Darius introduced himself.

"Joe," the man said.

Under questioning Joe revealed he was an Aleut, an Eskimo, and planted vegetables. "I come with the house like the books and furniture," he reported.

"What vegetables?"

"Beets. Asparagus."

"Who were the owners?"

"Farmers that got old."

"What crops did they plant?"

"Wheat. Always in a rush. Short growing season. You understand."

"Sure. But next autumn might arrive later than usual because the sun is hotter than normal."

"Less ice might help us catch more fish."

"Where do you live?"

"Close to the village. We are the proprietors of the general store."

Dahlia appeared, waving at Joe. She said to Darius, "Just met him yesterday. Seems nice enough. Breakfast is ready."

The two moved inside the house. Steaming bowls of porridge and a pitcher of cream sat on the table. Bacon and eggs fried on the stove.

"You purchased them - -"

"Joe's family's general store."

"Are we alone?"

"The others aren't up yet. Shall we eat? Enjoy yourself last night?"

Darius shrugged.

"You?"

"Maybe a little." She spread her manicured fingers, "The thing is - -"

"For God's sake, what?"

"I would have loved talking more with you - -"

"That's about what Wendy said."

"I don't want to sound like her."

"You could do worse. Go on."

"But Walter intruded and you went to bed so early. Sleep with her?"

"Negative."

"Good. I might have been jealous."

"Because you prefer me?"

"Respect is more appropriate. You're impressive."

"How?"

"As a scientist."

Darius sighed.

At the table they commenced to eat. Dahlia heaped cream on her porridge while saying, "When you spoke of the polar thingamabob, I believed you."

"Walter doubts me. Why not believe him?"

"His hairy legs disgust me."

"He made a pass?"

"Of course. I feared rape."

"He showed his - -"

"No. He begged me to strip."

She has a stunning body, Darius thought. Tight neck, pretty boobs, slim waist, narrow hips…her pubic hair must be russet…graceful legs.

"The bacon's burning!" Dahlia jumped up.

If only she weren't so emotional. Wendy, by contrast, is calm. If you made love to her in a haystack, she'd be knitting you a straw hat.

Wendy entered and Darius said, "I must get busy."

"How?"

"I need NTIS on line."

She read the blog over his shoulder:

NATIONAL TECHNICAL INFORMATION SERVICE

Geomagnetic polarity reversal.

Earth has problems with magnetic poles.

They won't stay put.

An impermanent solution.

Which way is North?

Terrestrial instability.

"Nothing new. I'll check the Intermagnet."

"What's that?"

A blog where magnetic specialists exchange info." He pressed keys.

INTERMAGNET

"Magnetic instability reported near the poles. Shouldn't last more than a day or two."

"Instability," Darius said. "The word describes human knowledge. It can't be relied on and we mustn't take unnecessary risks."

"A profound remark," Wendy said with admiration. "It implies we shouldn't count on certitudes."

"Right."

Intellectually, she and I are compatible, but likes repel, don't they?

Walter had joined the group, ignoring the conversation and the computer screen. Bolting down breakfast, he belched, patted his stomach and said, "I've eaten too much. I'm ready to leave for the village," Dahlia had agreed to take them.

"Same here," Wendy said.

They left the kitchen.

"In a while." Dahlia called and said to Darius, "Give me details about you."

He winced. "Well, I'm terminally shy."

"If you were sick at a railroad station, I'd describe that as a terminal illness." Dahlia shook her head and smiled. "But I don't care. When did you first get interested in magnetism?"

"By age eight I'd started to collect magnets, not just the ones you stack on refrigerator doors but fanciful ones I found in a catalog and persuaded my father to buy for me - - round, square and horseshoe magnets, magnets resembling animals - -"

"Why are you stopping?"

"I have - -"

"Continue, please"

"Well. I'm ashamed. As a kid, I murdered small animals with an air pistol."

"C'mon. You can't murder animals." Wendy rebuked him with laughing eyes.

Darius continued.

"Arrested?"

"For cruelty to animals."

"What happened next?"

"I was released in my mother's custody."

"O.K."

"And human figures which would seemingly, ah, copulate...though I failed to understand the word yet...and a unicorn whose tail and horn were magnetic poles."

"Gosh."

"The ancients believed magnets had souls."

"You too?"

Darius grinned. "Sometimes."

Before he could explain, Walter shouted. "We're all set."

#

The day was warmish for northwest Canada and the Humvee was equipped with a heater so they found themselves okay in a strange place. Dahlia finally parked. Dahlia sat back and listened.

"Shit," Darius said.

Dahlia eyeballed him. Then, her necklace fell off.

"What secured it?" Darius asked, face blank.

"A magnetic clasp."

Darius, was forced to wonder if there had been a miniscule magnetic surge. Impossible! He assured himself excitedly.

They discussed dinner. "I'll cook!" Wendy volunteered.

"I'll cook tomorrow." Walter promised.

"I'm next though I never learned how," Darius admitted, feeling stupid.

The neon sign read General Store and they entered. "What's good?" Dahlia asked the butcher she knew to be related to Joe and therefore an Aleut.

"Caribou. We're lucky to have it."

"Why?"

"The dumb-assed animals…they're called the Freemont Herd, a million strong when they peak once in a hundred years - -"

In his mind's eye, Darius saw a million humans their sense of direction lost, wandering the prairie.

"- - are migrating earlier than usual, and not south but north."

"Oh. Give me fifty pounds of caribou charged to my account. Walter?"

"As a s.o.b…" He chuckled.

"S.o.b?"

"Son of a butcher. My brother worked in his shop."

"So?"

The right side of Walter's lips looped down. "I shouldn't tell you - -"

"You must!"

"O.K. Sol, my older sibling, was, fuck...a pedophile. I swore him I'd never reveal his secret but I blackmailed him for a small amount of money. I was only a kid."

"Where is Sol?"

"Committed suicide. I love roast duck," Walter said coldly.

The butcher remarked, "They're migrating with the stupid caribou."

"Mallards or black?" Dahlia asked.

"Mallards," she said, not really caring.

"I'll buy a dozen ducks before they're gone."

"I can cook hot dogs," Darius seemed to brag.

"How <u>American</u>," Dahlia rejoined. "If you put in white wine and sauerkraut, you'd have <u>choucroute garnie</u>."

"French again."

"Ouí."

"I could cook that," Darius claimed.

"No. It's a gourmet's secret."

Wendy had wandered to a slot machine, pulled a handle and caterwauled, "I'm being screwed. I hit two cherries- -"

"Cherries. Remember when you had yours?" Walter tried to joke.

"You're a schizo," Wendy hissed. "The machine stopped.

Animals and birds migrating too early and in the wrong direction, a clasp that won't hold, a malfunctioning slot machine - - magnetic mischief must be responsible. If only these events were just mischief.

#

Having stowed the food in the Humvee, the four strolled to the dock where Joe, the gardener, chores evidently finished, inspected his marine equipment. He greeted them warmly.

"Some news. The oil guys are here for the day. In the hills." He pointed. "They're drilling."

"How deep?" Darius wondered.

"Don't know. Ask them."

A Ford truck had parked outside the store and the group came back. The three men were munching sandwiches.

Walter stepped up and demanded, "You're engineers?"

"Yeah, buddy. You?"

"A professor of EE."

"What's that?"

"Electrical engineering."

"O.K."

"How deep do you plan to drill?"

"Until we find black gold. This area could be another Prudhoe Bay."

"Off the north east coast of Canada," Walter reminded the group.

Darius said to the hardhats, "Intend to go down a mile?"

"Further if necessary."

"That puts you in spitting distance of the mantle which is two miles deep, the nearest you can get to the inner core."

"What's inside the inner core?'

"It's all molten iron though some speculate there might be a giant crystal formed from the pressure."

"A super diamond mine with tunnels leading in?"

"Science fiction." Although, he thought, sci-fi often turned out to be true. "Where was I? Before that, you'll come to the gabbred, a granite layer."

Gabbred, a boring word.

"O.K." No wonder the hardhats sounded bored.

"Could you attach a measuring device, a Teslometer…negative… too expensive. You'd need to weld the instrument to the drill."

"No reason why not. The company is keen on good p.r. and sir --"

"I'm Professor Gertz." I have credentials." Walter lit a cigarette with a match.

"All the better. The company will fly the gadget in."

The oilers departed and Darius went on. "A magnetometer might tell us how much the inner core accelerates. Inside it magnetic eddies form and when the southerly-pointed ones which have been building up outnumber the northernly-pointed ones, a polar swap takes place; the compass needle dips south."

"I want a second whack at the slot machine," Wendy said. The group went back inside and she inserted a coin. Again it jammed.

"We might be experiencing the miniscule effects of a magnetic surge," Darius said, aware that he repeated himself.

"The Eskimo family must have too." Dahlia said.

Nobody spoke until they returned to the house.

"What happened to them?"

"They were hunters as well as farmers. When up north they got lost in the woods and froze to death. How do I know this? One of them, I was told, kept a diary of his last days on earth."

"The hunters lacked a compass?" Darius queried.

"Dumped it. Defective."

"Not defective," Darius said with a little moan. "Messed up because of altered magnetism." He glanced at Dahlia and felt twitch in his groin. Out of character. Next thing, he'd turn aggressive.

At the identical moment, Wendy touched his arm and smiled, invitingly. Darius looked at her askance and she examined Walter who inspected Dahlia who ignored him, gazing toward Darius.

A perfect circle. He batted his blond eyelashes and said, "We're also screwed up. A hot meal might help."

"Meal is for animals," Dahlia rebuked him. "You mean dinner."

"And I'm the chef," Wendy wailed, getting the caribou steaks that Dahlia had placed in the freezer.

"I'll mash the spuds," Walter grumbled.

"We need a balanced diet," Wendy said, "Vegetables?'

"Only in cans," Dahlia said. She put an electric can opener on the counter, and pressed a button.

Walter watched. "It's revolving in the wrong direction. The blade won't cut." He proved it with canned tomatoes which he opened, using a manual opener.

Wanting to escape, Darius planted a clumsy kiss on Dahlia's lips and she fled.

#

Again they drank cocktails in the livingroom and sat before the TV. Among the disasters reported were several airplane accidents with pilot error blamed.

Walter fumed, "Fuck! Could be instruments were at fault."

"Have you ever crashed?"

"Sure. During a windstorm. I was flying my own plane and the altimeter informed me I was much higher than proved to be the case. Hard to gauge at dusk. I escaped without injuries."

"Were you alone?"

Walter chewed his tongue and finally said, "The woman was killed."

"Who was she?"

"A casual friend."

"How casual?"

"Did I screw her? I reckon."

"Married at the time?"

"Uh-huh."

"You're promiscuous," Dahlia accused him of.

"At last I'm not anti-miscuous. A joke."

Wendy blinked. "I wouldn't object just so it's me he's with."

Dahlia frowned. "I'd object if it were me."

They watched a commercial for a new skin product, Saveeno, offering "100 percent protection from the sun."

Dahlia declared, "I wouldn't buy the gunk. Must make you ugly."

"You're too beautiful to get ugly," Walter asserted.

Wendy demurred. "He exaggerates."

"Correction. Embellishes. Fudges the facts," Darius said.

Dahlia carried the salad. " Vinaigrette dressing. Two-thirds olive oil, the rest vinegar with a trace of garlic."

Dahlia's a hedonist, Darius thought. Loves food and, I imagine, sex. Is she my opposite? If so, I'm anhedonistic…don't experience pleasure…which isn't the case.

They masticated in silence.

"I'm almost full," Darius complained.

"But you've hardly eaten anything. You're too thin. You should eat more," Dahlia coaxed.

"You sound like his ma," Wendy said. "Or his wife."

"Here we go again," Dahlia said. "You're jealous."

"Right. Darius was attracted to me. Now it's you."

"Walter belonged to me, now he ogles you."

"Want to be the mother of his child?" Wendy asked.

"I can't decide."

"Maybe we should swap bedrooms."

"Perhaps," Dahlia said with a ghost of a smile.

They glanced at the men who listened.

"Want the caribou bloody, medium or charred?"

They opted for medium, seemingly hedging their bets.

#

Wendy served the steaks, Walter the mashed potatoes and Dahlia hoisted her glass. "To us!" Wine glasses clinked.

They sliced their steaks. All were well-done "I voted for medium," Walter said.

"Ditto," said Dahlia.

Darius said," Fine by me." He chewed. The caribou meat was lean, tender and unlike the ordinary caribou, he supposed, it must have eaten moss and lichen.

"Ditto," Wendy repeated. She tasted the mashed potatoes. "Filled with lumps."

"Won't kill you," Walter said cheerfully.

Dahlia seemed to remember. "You said I'm not beautiful."

"But," Darius noted, "Walter has a character flaw. He can't avoid hyperbole."

"Misrepresentation?"

"Yes. Nonetheless, in one respect he was accurate - - instrument failure on the plane."

"Correct," Walter said.

"When did the accident happen?"

"Recently."

"Then it occurred for the identical reason the hunters froze - - hypermagnetism."

"But that implies hypermagnetism is everywhere."

"Just now and then and too erratic to be proved."

"This conversation makes me nervous, " Wendy said.

"Dessert will soothe you," Darius said. "I'll scoop the ice cream. Where is it?"

"In the fridge," Dahlia said. They regarded each other awkwardly. "Bottom drawer."

Impossible not to hear the sexuality in her throaty voice and Walter reacted. "Whom do you prefer? The short man or me?"

"Time will tell, I think."

"And I?" Wendy said, shifting her gaze from Darius to Walter.

"I-I-I, "Darius stuttered. "All you think of is yourselves. It makes me edgy."

"Does anything else exist?"

"The world, Walter. Our world. On the cusp of succumbing to skin cancer, blindness and disorientation."

"Because of a geomagnetic reversal? To repeat, I'm doubtful."

"The proof must be in this room," Darius insisted.

"What proof?"

"People change."

"That's natural."

"But how much? You dug Dahlia?"

"O.K."

"Now Wendy?"

Walter looked at Wendy and winked.

"This isn't a parlor game. Dahlia was attracted to you. Maybe it's me now."

Walter sort of harrumphed. "Let's ask the girls."

"Women," said Dahlia. "A male chauvinist."

"You said that before."

"I mean it more than ever."

"See?" Darius crowed.

"Handsome, though," Wendy stated.

"How does Dahlia feel?"

She said, "Darius is witty."

"Yeah," Walter said. He conned us into believing we've reversed our affections...we haven't...to prove his theory."

"Enough of this," Dahlia said. "O.K., Walter?"

He nodded.

She said, "Any port in a storm, huh, Darius?"

"I don't wish to discuss it yet. Tomorrow, O.K.? He inspected the freezer drawer. "Vanilla, pistachio, strawberry, chocolate."

"White, green, red. brown--the colors of an African flag," Wendy jested. "I'll take chocolate."

"Vanilla for me," Walter said. "The opposite."

"I'll have strawberry," said Darius.

"Pistachio," Dahlia murmured, "symbolizing the green environment, what Darius is concerned with."

His mind was akin a camera, recording everything. LIKES ATTRACT, he said and put his arm around her slender waist.

Wendy eyeballed Walter and ran out. OPPOSITES REPEL, he saw.

"Enough for this evening," he said and turned in.

Chapter Four

THAT NIGHT THE WIND rose and the window in Darius' room rattled. It could have been a hurricane except they were too far north. Then the entire house shuddered. Was he having a bad dream? He got up and walked to the hall. Should he knock on Wendy's door? No. She'd suppose he was making a pass. He would be alone during the scary night.

Unable to sleep, he paced in the bedroom, eager for dawn which finally came. He witnessed the pale sky filled with golden blurs. Was he the only person to view the scene? His camera-mind recorded it. A prelude to a polar swap or a product of his vivid imagination? Perhaps he'd never know. Exhausted, Darius slept.

#

But not for long. No one else was awake. Grabbing a glass of milk from the fridge, he rushed outside; wearing a windbreaker borrowed from the coat rack in the hall. He went to the garage where Dahlia kept the Humvee. Bicycles stood beside it. Darius pedaled to the village, searching for what?

Some kind of answer.

At the general store Darius encountered Joe who reported he'd just been fishing. Through the plate glass windows brightly-painted sloops could be seen, nets draped from their bows.

"A big catch?" Darius asked.

"No. Forced to head back. Wind gusts."

"Notice a change in the sky?"

Joe hesitated, "But you wouldn't believe me."

"Still, talk."

"Splotches of golden stuff."

"High in the sky?"

"Yup, boss."

Joe went to the house to resume gardening and Darius plunked down a dollar for a bad mug of coffee that he slowly drank at the Formica counter. He felt morose. A possible cataclysm loomed but he could prove zilch.

Although an atheist he prayed. A contradiction? Desperate people pray and this time the prayer had been answered. Joe had also witnessed the golden blurs. He (Darius) would persist.

The oilers' truck parked in front of the store and the guys entered. Seeing one Darius said, "We got the gizmo."

"The magnetometer?"

"Uh-huh. We'll fasten it to the diamond drill."

"Excellent. How long before you reach the mantle?"

"Coupla days."

Elated, a sensation he seldom experienced, Darius returned to the house. The now plausible polar flip-flop might explain the group's shifting sexual preferences.

Inside the house, Dahlia said, "Where have you been?"

He recounted that morning's adventures.

"Joe and you saw what? Unbelievable." She paused and said, "But I've concluded I truly love you."

Reluctantly...the golden blurs were more important...he said, "Instead of Walter?"

"Yes."

"You never loved him?"

"Oh, at first, maybe a little."

"Fuck him?" I'm out of character once more.

"Nope."

"Should I take you at your word?"

"You lack a choice."

"Wendy's perspective?"

"Ask her," Dahlia said.

The Japanese-American woman came downstairs, body and head wrapped in a towel, shoulders naked. "I was washing my hair."

"Wendy, tell Darius how you feel."

"About?"

"Walter and him."

"Differently at different times."

"Your emotions change a lot?"

"Constantly."

"Any notion why?"

"Assuming Darius is correct as regards a polar turn-around, I'll present a neurological response. The human brain has two hemispheres, left and right. The question Darius seeks to answer is, what would happen if the hemispheres reversed functions - - their electrical currents might reverse; and with them our emotions."

"Sounds like emotional turbulence."

"Mercurial is more apt."

"Teen-age emotional swings?"

"Sure."

Walter entered the room, "You're referring to me?"

"We're talking about everything and nothing."

"Doesn't that describe the universe?"

"You're a pessimist."

Walter smiled. "I'd rather shock people like an electric eel."

"Sounds fishy," Darius said.

"Walter must have a sense of humor after all," Dahlia said.

"I appreciate that."

"Thanks. I'm fond of you."

Wendy demonstrated anger by pursing her lips. "I figured you were attracted to me."

"Both. Both."

"I'm not the sort of person who shares partners."

"In the past?"

"She - - I don't care to discuss the matter. Besides, I'm straight now."

"For how long?"

"Forever, Walter." Tears welled from Wendy's Asian eyes.

"It's a minor matter," Dahlia said, staring at Walter.

"But it's not," Darius said. As she herself suggested, her emotions might reverse during a polar swap."

Walter bellowed, "There's still no proof such an event will occur."

THREE

Chapter Five

For the next few days nothing happened. Zero. They went to the store, cooked, ate, watched TV, drank wine, and slept. That was it.

Darius would have been bored except for his obsessive interest in what occurred at the farmhouse. Behavioral changes, including his own, might presage a magnetic catastrophe.

When something happened, it did with bewildering speed.

First, the oilers came to the store while he was shopping and reported the magnetometer fastened to their drill had given a strange reading. Puzzled, he put the numbers on the Intermagnet and waited for other scientists to respond. Finally they produced results. Scanning them he experienced utter alarm. Their calculations indicated a geomagnetic polarity reversal might take place as soon as late summer or early autumn.

He put his findings on the Intermagnet, but no one responded.

At last one did.

"Professor Alphonso Jackson here. Are you reading me?"

Darius knew who Jackson was, a white-haired black man, a convert to

Judaism, after winning the National Science Award for his work in advanced mathematics and micro-gravity.

On the computer, Darius typed, "An honor to receive your message, sir."

Jackson typed, "Having reviewed your numbers, I agree: a geomagnetic polarity reversal might occur as soon as late summer or early fall - -"

Yes, only three scant months from now! He read on.

"There is, though, a 90% possibility of error."

Why? Maybe Jackson and other establishment scientists couldn't confront the truth but took the position of watchful waiting as if the world had prostate cancer.

Could humans suffer the same fate as the dinos? The notion, he realized, might be construed as a neurotic fixation. He wished he'd been trained as a bio-scientist.

What made matters worse was that a polar swap might coincide with the Northern Lights...the Aurora Borealis...and delay recognition of the danger: when the poles changed places the magnetic field would temporarily weaken and stop protecting us from the solar wind which would enter the atmosphere and bombard our bodies with potentially lethal particles, destroying our cells on the atomic level. No form of life could survive except maybe fungus spores, protected by a coating. Even Intermagnet scientists failed to grasp the implications.

Darius discussed these questions with the group. Walter, per usual, scoffed.

"You're demented, Sykes. What potentially lethal particles? And the dinos, as you persist in calling them, perished not because of a polar swap but for the simple reason they couldn't adapt to a new environment, being stupid creatures."

"And we're not?"

"No. Perhaps misguided, like you."

"What about the concurrent Northern Lights?"

"Just bad luck. And you're confused regarding the reversal."

"Won't happen, huh?"

"You've heard my views before."

"Would you participate in an experiment?"

"Describe it."

"I'm convinced we're surrounded by magnetic eddies too small for an ordinary compass to register but nonetheless powerful enough to influence our behavior. I propose we keep mental notes on how we change."

He himself would use his mental camera.

"Nothing wrong with that."

"Oh yes there is," Wendy said with excitement. "We might not remember how we react, or our synapses could be clouded."

"Mine is clear as a bell," Dahlia interjected.

"So you think," Darius warned.

"You're gloomy. You haven't changed."

"Wait." He laughed.

"This is the new you!" Dahlia lunged at him.

He said, "Walter might be jealous."

Walter frowned and looked at Wendy who said, "I'm fond of you."

"How fond?"

"Bedfond."

"Well - -" Darius raised his eyebrows. "Wendy has changed which proves my theory."

"It doesn't quite," Wendy said. "I'm bedfond of Darius too."

"You sound like a fucking whore!" Dahlia exploded.

"She's generally cool," Darius reminded them. "She's becoming her opposite, indicating I'm correct."

"Indicates is far from actual facts," Walter said, voice gentle.

"Walter has also degnahc…changed," Darius pointed out. "Which means we all have. The question is a how much."

"No," Wendy again corrected. "The important question is, are the changes temporary or permanent?"

"Tell with time," Dahlia said.

"What?"

"Time will tell, I intended to say. I need a nap before dinner."

While she slept, Wendy discussed magnetotherapy.

"Why do Indian customs dictate that we sleep with our head to the north and why do we fast on full moon days? Most of these ancient customs have a scientific basis: The earth is a huge magnet with its magnetic lines of force that has a direct impact on us. Our body is also invested with magnetism and enveloped in a magnetic field. The strongest magnetic field is created by the brain while we sleep and sleeping with our head to the north facilitates the easy flow of the earth's magnetism through our body thus inducing sound sleep. The age-long custom of fasting on full moon days can also probably be explained. During a full moon our body fluids flow with greater ease and so fasting on these days helps maintain an equilibrium of liquids in the body. We are affected by the dark and bright phases of the moon because every planet through its magnetism exercises some influence on other planets.

"The story of magnetism goes back a long way to many centuries before Christ. The earliest mention of the magnet as a healing agent, however, is one of the four Vedas on the treatise of medicine – the *Atharvaveda*. The ancient Egyptians were also apparently familiar with the properties of magnetic forces as they utilized it to preserve mummies. Their legendary beauty, Cleopatra, was said to have worn a tiny magnet on her forehead- probably to preserve her charms. Most civilizations, however, invested the magnet with magical powers. They wore magnets as amulets or charms to relieve aches and pains – its healing properties were used unwittingly.

"It was not until the beginning of the 16th century that magnets became an object of scientific research. A Swiss alchemist and physician, Paracelsus, discovered its healing powers. Other researchers took the cue from him. Dr. Samuel Hahneman, the father of homeopathy, was fully convinced of the magnet's healing powers and recommended its use but magnetotherapy is now widely recognized and has scientific support.

She paused.

"What's the matter?"

"I'm out of breath."

"Continue," Walter urged.

"Magnetotherapy is very effective in drawing out pain and relieving stiffness as when the body comes into contact with magnets. The magnetic waves pass through the tissues and induce secondary currents which produce impacting beats, thus reducing pains and swellings. It also revives and promotes the growth of cells and increases the number of healthy red blood corpuscles. The red corpuscles contain hemoglobin which contain iron. The magnets influence the iron in the blood through which it reaches every part of the body removing calcium, cholesterol and other deposits- it cleans, purifies and ionizes the blood, ionized blood flows easily thus there is no clotting, eases the activity of the heart and normalizes blood pressure. The secretion of hormones is also regulated and this improves the luster of the skin.

"Magnetotherapy requires no medicines, no injections, no tonics. Just magnets! Magnets of various shapes, sizes and strengths are used to regulate and strengthen the natural system and preserve the balance of magnetic field in the body. Two types of artificial magnets are used: Electro-magnets and permanent magnets. Electro-magnets work only when connected to electricity. Permanent magnets are fully charged with electric current and remain permanently magnetized. They are made of an alloy called alnico composed of aluminum, nickel, iron and cobalt in different proportions. For most treatments disc shaped magnets of medium or high potency (1500-3000 gauss power) are generally used. These discs are usually sold in pairs – north pole and south pole. The two poles possess different therapeutic properties. The north pole magnet is effective in diseases caused by bacterial infection and the south pole is used to treat all kinds of pains, swellings and weakness. Treatment is either local or general. In local treatment the selected pole is applied directly on the affected area or placed nearest to the spot if it is sensitive or painful. If both poles are required, the main magnet is placed on the ailing sort and the second under the palm or sole on the same side. When the whole body is affected general treatment is necessary."

"O.K."

"Both poles are placed under the palms or soles. The north pole is applied to right side and the south pole to the left. The north is also generally applied to the upper and front side. For uneven parts – forehead, eyes, ears, cheeks, throat, wrists, etc. – ceramic, crescent shaped magnets of a lower potency (400-500 gauss power) are available.

"Each session in magnetotherapy lasts for twenty – thirty minutes. Initially, magnets are applied for five minutes just once a day and gradually increasing to twenty – thirty minutes twice a day depending upon the individual. Treatment can continue even after complete cure to preserve general health. In fact, even normal, healthy people are advised to apply magnets for ten minutes daily to keep fit. Magnetized water is also strongly recommended. This is the only prescribed medication and acts as a tonic. Besides water, other liquids – milk, fruit juice, hair and skin oils- can also be magnetized. All one has to do is place two-liter jugs of water on the two poles of disc magnets of three thousand gauss power for twelve to twenty four hours. For regular use five - six hours is adequate. The water can be stored in separate bottles labeled north and south and some of it can be mixed and labeled bio-polar. Two ounces twice a day is prescribed for adults and one ounce for children. The dose can be diluted with water if it causes dryness. Magnetotherapy has proved especially effective in curing digestive and nervous disorders and relieving aches and pains especially rheumatism, migraines, arthritis etc. There are no side effects but nevertheless there are some guidelines to be considered.

"I should add a strong magnet placed near the temple causes spots before the eyes and the loss of equilibrium."

"What?"

"Hah! The dinos," Darius said.

"Finally, the magcap. Weak magnets embedded in the cloth causes headaches to vanish. Ecomagnetism - - "

#

The clock read six-thirty p.m., a half-hour later than normal, when they gathered for cocktails in the living room.

"Remember saying 'tell with time'?" Darius asked Dahlia.

"Never said that."

"In your case I suspect the changes are permanent."

"How dire! You haven't changed after all. I prefer Walter."

Darius knew it sounded childish but couldn't help himself when he answered "I love Wendy now."

She said, "Darius is mine - - temporarily."

He observed, "Two temporary, two permanent, an inconclusive result."

"As I anticipated zero proof a polar swap is happening."

"Still, we might reverse Walter," Dahlia said. "And that would make Darius correct."

"Oh dear," Wendy remonstrated. "Even I, a neurologist, fail to comprehend."

"Simple," said Darius. "Opposites attract, likes repel. Or is it the other way around?"

Dahlia said, "There ought to be a magnetic dating service that matches up opposites with questionnaires. An e-ynomrah - -"

"E-Harmony, she means," Wendy said. "I mentioned ecomagnetic... ecologically friendly cap...would create a friendly environment for sex. At least I hope so."

After awhile Dahlia suggested, "Let's have dinner. I don't recall who's supposed to cook. I choose Darius."

#

No one had bothered to shop so he ransacked the fridge for things to eat and came up with a concoction he named trash hash.

"Consisting of?"

Darius responded by placing the food on the table - - caribou, celery, eggs, bacon, milk, red peppers, flour.

"Ugh," Dahlia mouthed.

"It will taste good." He lifted a cleaver.

"Aren't you right-handed?"

"Yes. Why?"

"You're using your left."

"Oh." He switched hands and set the table - -glasses on the right, spoons on the left.

"The reverse of where they should be," Dahlia scolded. "Which hand do you favor, Walter?"

"The left. I'm a southpaw."

"Shake hands with me."

Walter extended his right hand.

"You're a northpaw now."

The engineer seemed puzzled. "I can't account for that."

"Further proof of a polar swap?" Darius said with a triumphant smile. "As if one were needed."

"Perhaps I've suddenly become ambidextrous." Walter lapsed into silence.

"Are you telling the truth?" Dahlia asked defiantly.

"Yeah, yeah."

Employing his left hand, Darius mixed the hash. "We haven't heard from the ladies. "Right or left?"

"I'm a Republican," Dahlia announced. "A righty."

"I'm a Socialist," Wendy reported. "A lefty."

Darius sighed. "I meant your hands."

"I masturbate with the right."

"Left for me."

"So, Dahlia's right-handed, Wendy left. I'm right-handed, Walter left, at least before we transposed. Dahlia right, me too. Likes repel, opposites attract. We're incompatible as are Walter and Wendy.

"You're forgetting we could change back," Wendy objected.

"That would amount to the same."

Wendy looked at Dahlia. "But we're compatible," she cooed.

Dahlia frowned and tasted the hash. "Awful. I want to vomit." She gazed at Wendy, implicitly rejecting her.

#

After dinner they went to the livingroom and Dahlia served the cognac she'd brought from Chicago. Nobody wished to watch TV... the images of skin cancer and blindness depressed them...so the conversation returned to politics.

"You're a Republican and understand the Darth Vader aspect of politics, Walter."

"And you're a Socialist because you're stupidly rational."

"Stupid, yeah, but in possession of a Ph.D."

"Naive then."

"That's a Republican cliché."

"Most politics consist of clichés, disguised as appeals to emotions," Darius noted. "Politicians seek to reach the common man."

Belching, Walter sipped cognac. "What is the common man? Also a cliché isn't it?"

"Everything is clichéd now."

"Why?"

"Blame advertising and its kissing cousin, TV. They give us noise but little content. Even the small helping of news is half-baked!"

"Unlike you to get angry," Dahlia said. "You're normally calm."

"I can't be calm about politics. Drives me nuts."

"I agree," Wendy said.

"You don't have nuts, being female," Walter said with a hint of scorn.

"A bad joke," judged Dahlia.

"Male chauvinism again, "Wendy said to Walter.

"Something deeply hidden has to lie behind things," Darius said, "I'm paraphrasing Albert Einstein."

"What things?"

"Perhaps magnetic things. The subject obsessed him in the manner I'm obsessed by the unknowableness of the universe. It's a mystery we can't fathom. Nor could Einstein who was unable to fit magnetism into his unified field theory...an attempt to explain the universe with a single mathematical formula...but failed. Like me."

"Are we under magnetic influence...call it a spell...right now?" Dahlia asked.

"Hypermagnetism? Yes."

"Then we should be forgiven for acting abnormally." She removed her blouse, exposing small nipples.

"Want to compete?" Wendy said, ripping off her sweater and unhooking her bra. She had larger breasts than Dahlia.

Walter eyed them. "I dig big mammaries."

Darius thought, the same as before. Walter attracted to Wendy now instead of Dahlia. He swings to and fro...fro and to...as do I. Magnetism must be changing constantly. No wonder the dinos were confused, helpless. At least they weren't juvenile like us.

But he felt compelled to say, "I prefer small ones."

Dahlia beamed. "I adore smallish men."

Wendy smirked. "Tall men are superior."

"I'm grateful," Walter said, bestowing a lascivious smile.

Under it, Wendy fell into his arms. "Bedfond," she whispered.

Darius had been recording with his mental camera. Abruptly the scene changed. Walter leered at Dahlia and Wendy touched Darius' crotch.

#

He was alarmed. Frivolity concerned them instead of vital matters.

As a believer in civil liberties and democratic (small "d" government), he found himself appalled by our nation's happiness resorting to war, disregard of the Geneva Convention, willingness to inflict collateral damage (a euphemism), use torture, make lying routine, get increasingly assertive and bellicose, engage in exaggeration, force patriotism down our throats, turn hypocrisy into an art, disguise militarism as a search for peace. Immorality had become S.O.P. with our government.

Its aims were: reverse <u>Roe v. Wade</u> and allow states to ban abortion. Expand executive power. End racial preferences designed to assist African-Americans, speed executions. Welcome religion into public life.

Why? The important question. Was America (another not- quite-a-lie word because America meant North America and included Mexico and Canada, The United States was correct) fundamentally dishonest? Beginning with boosterism, a 19th century term, intended to lure settlers into the mid-west (now the heartland.) Were we flawed by too much ambition or our DNA? At any rate, he concluded, the American empire, having swiftly risen, verged on collapse.

Darius opened his eyes. Had he dozed? Too much wine? Things had returned to normal.

Fully clothed, the Japanese-American woman said, "I've been making a fool of myself."

Dahlia said, "Me too."

"And I," Walter grumbled. "What was the argument about? Oh yes, hypermagnetism which couldn't possibly exist."

"But it could," Wendy countered.

The electrical engineer answered, "Not nearly powerful enough."

From the kitchen they heard rattling which stopped fast.

"I'll look." Dahlia returned almost at once. "The pots and pans are stuck together."

They rushed to the kitchen.

"You're strong, Walter. Tear them apart." Dahlia challenged.

He grinned, then, muscles straining and covered with sweat, struggled to separate a pair of conjoined cast-iron frying pans. "Can't do it," he admitted finally.

Darius inspected a drawer - - the knives, forks and spoons weren't stuck.

"Pewter," he said. "No ferrous metal."

The frying pans separated.

"The magnetic episode has ended," Darius declared. "We've learned a lot."

"Such as?" Walter queried.

"A harbinger of the future. Hypermagnetism threatens to overwhelm us."

Wendy nodded. "Suppose it affects our bodies? Red blood cells consist partly of iron. We could be magnetized as might have happened to the dog!"

"How?"

"Hemoglobin is important to bind both oxygen and carbon dioxide to the red blood cells and it is a metaloprotein attached to red blood cells. The chance binding of carbon dioxide is two hundred times more likely than with oxygen. Red blood cells generally survive in the blood stream for ninety days and are replaced continually during that interval. Degeneration of the red blood cells can cause muscle pain and even leukemia."

"Meaning?" Darius said.

"Guess."

"Magnetism, of course."

"You still don't accept my position?" Walter asked.

At that moment Darius felt toward Wendy a pang of love. She'd taken his side. "Negative." he said. "I'm convinced a polar swap is coming soon."

"You have further proof?"

"We're beginning to speak in reverse."

"Show me."

"It only happens now and then. Wait."

#

They waited. Finally, Dahlia arrived.

"Cramps," she said. "My period."

"When did you have it last?"

"I can't recall. Recently, I believe."

"What product did you use when menstruating?"

"Tampons. Brought them from Chicago."

"Is the tampon box full?"

"Some are gone."

"So you have had periods?"

Dahlia blinked. "I suppose."

"You can't blame magnetism for irregularity," Walter asserted.

"True," Darius said. "But her sense of time may be out of kilter. Another symptom of a reversal."

"Sey," Wendy said. "Backspeak…speaking backwards…may be another."

"It must be. We lack a better explanation."

"Signifying our brain hemispheres are reversing." Wendy insisted.

"And spelling backwards," Darius said. He wrote his name on a scrap of paper, SEKYS. "Maybe I'm turning dyslexic again."

It remained early and Walter wanted to go out. Dahlia said she hated driving after sunset so Walter sat behind the wheel.

"To where?" Wendy asked.

"The tavern must be open. The Eskimos need something to do at night when they can't fish or hunt. And they lack TV, in their homes, I bet," Walter said.

"Is this an excuse for getting drunk?" Dahlias said.

"I'll stick to beer."

The Humvee halted before the tavern. Inside, Eskimos wearing suspenders packed the pub, named NNE. A sloe-eyed waitress arrived at their wooden booth with initials carved on the table and leather seats. It was supported by tusks.

"What animals are they from?" Darius questioned.

"Walruses."

While they waited for their orders, he examined the interior.

Walls of varnished plywood on which hung caribou, deer and other trophy horns, plus plaques bearing stuffed fish - - tuna, sharks, salmon and lake trout.

"No whales?" he joked.

She took him seriously. "Too big."

"What about Santa Claus?"

"Lives north of here."

"Bring you gifts?"

"No."

"Why is this place named NNE?"

"The direction of the North Pole."

Darius cogitated: if the poles shift the tavern would have to change its appellation.

He ordered bottled water, Dahlia and Wendy soda pop, and Walter bourbon with a beer chaser. "Also a pack of Camels."

"A cigarette smoker!" Dahlia said.

"Now and then."

"Then is now. Have you smoked, Darius?"

"Never. Nicotine is - - "

"Addictive. I wouldn't take the risk. You Wendy?"

"Several packs a day when she and I broke up. If Walter smokes, I must too."

Darius thought, Walter and Wendy are alike in regards to smoking. The same with Dahlia and me.

The waitress brought the drinks, the Camels and a matchbook with NNE printed on it. Walter opened the pack and lit his and Wendy's cigarettes.

He remarked, "I only smoked because, during my divorce, I became anxious about dough. The fucking judge gave her alimony."

"You were rich compared to her?" Dahlia inquired.

"MIT paid me well, and she was just a housewife."

Wendy bridled. "Just a housewife? She expected to have children?"

Walter nodded and demanded more bourbon. He said to Dahlia, "If you and I married, I could manage your stock portfolio. I have an insight -- "

"Go on." Dahlia didn't seem interested.

"Stockbrokers make money on each trade whether the stock goes up or down. If they hedge their bets by selling short...betting against the same stocks they buy...in a lower proportion, they almost have to turn a profit when their commissions are added to the mix."

"So?"

"We buy a brokerage business."

"Why do I need you?"

"I'm an expert in everything."

"Marriage too?"

"Well - -" He ordered a third bourbon.

Dahlia looked at him. "An alcoholic?"

"I was before I joined AA but I fell off the wagon."

"Now?"

"Under control mostly. I deserve a reprieve." He gulped the bourbon, then the chaser.

"You'll get fat," Dahlia warned.

The joint was noisy with Eskimos crowding the bar and yelling at the bartender. Electric fans twirled on the corrugated tin ceiling.

Suddenly, silence. A man emerged through the swinging doors. He wore a long, black coat and carried a bible. A few Eskimos dropped to their knees.

"He's a preacher," the waitress informed them.

"They must be converts," Dahlia said, "Does he reside here?"

"No. He moves from village to village."

"An itinerant evangelist," Darius noted. "He's a creationist – rejects Darwin." His name?"

"Jeremy," the sloe-eyed woman said.

Jeremy removed his coat, revealing a cross draped on his neck. Below that a cassock.

"He resembles a magician," Wendy said.

As if to prove her right, he drew a pointed hat from the cassock.

"It might require magic to save us," Darius was saying.

At the identical moment Jeremy shouted, "Only God can save us."

"Hallelujah!" some Aleuts said.

"The preacher has a following," Darius observed.

Jeremy went on, "God is light!"

"Like the sun at noon," Darius muttered.

"We must become true believers."

"In a polar swap," Darius added.

Walter hiccupped. "I disagree."

"God shall save the world."

"From disorientation," Darius said.

"I'm getting woozy," Walter admitted.

"We ought to go home," Wendy urged.

"I have a dream. Big-busted blondes in brothels," Walter laughed.

"Just like other men."

"God is great."

"But not enough," Darius said.

"Are you an atheist?" Dahlia wondered.

"Sey."

"What?" Dahlia cried.

"Yes, I meant."

"You, Wendy?"

"The same."

"Not me," Dahlia said. "I'm an Episcopal, high church.

like a Catholic. Walter!"

"A semi-Semite as I said. The Christian half of me believes in the devil."

"Two atheists, two not. We're divided per usual," Dahlia said.

"Sey," Walter said. "I meant yes."

"God, God, God, God," Jeremy bellowed.

"Time to leave," Dahlia ordered.

The rest of the group complied.

#

Back at the farmhouse nobody uttered another word until Wendy said, "I want to read a book."

Dahlia pointed at a shelf in the livingroom and Wendy pulled out a dusty volume, examining the title. "I can interpret it," she said. "Erehwon, nowhere spelled backwards."

"Where would the Eskimos find such a book?" Dahlia wondered.

"They must have visited Juneau or Nome."

"I've perused the book," Darius said, "A utopia by Samuel Butler."

"Yes," Dahlia remarked. "You mentioned utopias."

"Everybody wants one, including the farmers. An agraratopia," Wendy said.

"Not anymore," Darius answered. "Modern Americans are too preoccupied to dream of a better world."

"Should we assume we're headed nowhere?" Wendy asked.

"Depends on what happens."

#

Up early, Darius met Wendy in the kitchen.

"We're the atheists," she told him.

"So it appears. Further proof the two of us are alike."

"I remember. But likes repel."

"Dahlia and Walter aren't atheists. They're also alike."

"No opposites then. Nobody in our group attracts each other."

"Oh?" she said.

"How do you feel about me?"

"The question is your personal magnetism which ebbs and flows."

"At this moment?"

"Strong." She edged closer, "Ssik em."

"What?"

"Kiss me, I meant."

"I think you're speaking in reverse."

"You as well. 'Sey' instead of yes."

"Blame the augmented magnetism, a symptom."

#

"Sey," Wendy said. "Backspeak...speaking backwards...may be another."

"It must be."

"Signifying our brain hemispheres are reversing," Wendy insisted.

Dahlia examined her Rolex. "Breakfast."

#

While they ate, the oilers' truck parked before the house and a hardhat knocked on the door. Dahlia opened.

"Hey. I noticed you at the store. What's up?"

"Ma'am?"

"You seem embarrassed!"

"We need to drill here."

"Why, for God's sake?"

"We believe a major oil deposit may lie under your property." He pointed at the rig, 20 feet tall.

"Ugh." Dahlia said. "It will destroy my flower beds."

Darius joined them. "And they'll be using the magnetometer. I'll be able to read the results. I'll soon know if a polar swap is near."

"If I let them drill, oil pouring out on my land would be hideous."

With Wendy behind him Walter came and said, "You'll get a cut of the profits."

"What do I care? I own shares in the oil company."

"You'll be even richer. I envy you."

Dahlia said vaguely, "And I you - - "

"Don't. I'm Wendy's opposite."

Darius saw in his mind's eye: Wendy + Walter.

He wanted to see: Dahlia + Darius so he said, "Money fails to interest me." And it was the case.

Dahlia said to the hardhats, "Where do you plan to drill?"

"In your front yard."

"Shit."

By the time they'd finished breakfast, the oilers had begun installing their equipment.

#

"Worried" Wendy said to Dahlia.

"Yes. The reason you ask?"

"You have facial lines that weren't there before."

"Deep?"

"Superficial."

"Good. I'm too young to start getting old." She hastened to a mirror and fingered her face. "Lines around my mouth and under my eyes."

"Crow's feet, they call them."

"Signifying?"

"An inner conflict. Fess up."

"I can't yas."

"Yas?"

"Say, I meant."

Wendy turned to the men. "She's fighting the urge to speak backwards."

"What gives her this urge?" Walter said.

"Brain hemispheres must be involved. I can't explain yhw."

"Huh?"

"Why, that is."

"The answer has to be a ralop paws." Darius quickly corrected himself. "Polar swap."

"Ralop paws," Wendy repeated. "Sounds benign."

"If only it were," Darius said with a sigh. "What if everybody spoke backwards?"

"They already do," Walter smiled.

"Even about the niks - - "

"Skin," Dahlia said. "And now you too have lines on your face."

"Like uoy?" Wendy screamed. "I said you, didn't I?" A line appeared on her upper lip.

"We'd ought to stop talking," Darius said.

#

Silence.

Minutes later, from outside, a grinding noise.

The group rushed into the front yard.

"Struck oil?" Dahlia asked a hardhat.

"Too soon to tell," he responded.

"What if you don't find oil?"

"We'll go on drilling."

"With the magnetometer," Darius insisted.

"Yeah."

Joe, the Aleut, joined them. "What's that?"

"A gizmo that measures magnetism," a hardhat said.

"If it goes up?"

"Augmented magnetism would spell trouble," Darius declared.

"Woh?"

"He means how," Wendy said.

"We'll need a translator if this continues," Walter said.

"Better to study the phenomenon scientifically," Darius counseled.

"Ho - - I meant oh."

"We should have a magnetic laboratory."

"Where?"

"In the farmhouse, Dahlia. Walter and I will serve as architects."

"Your qualifications?"

"Both of us love good design." He and Walter stared at the women.

#

At the kitchen table, the engineer sketched plans for a magnetic laboratory - - Maglab, Darius termed it.

"On the roof," Walter suggested. "No. Won't bear the weight."

"The second story?"

"Too small."

"Ground floor?"

"Spoil the view," Dahlia complained.

"O.K., the basement."

"And?"

"Will require boxing gloves."

"Good," Walter said. "I always won when I boxed. And?"

"Now the details. Darius?"

He provided them. "We'll need a Faraday Cage - - "

"Cage?"

"A tin envelope to protect us from the adverse effects of hypermagnetism such as leukemia."

"And?"

"I need to inspect my wine cellar," Dahlia said and departed to the basement. She returned. "It must have been a repair place for the farmer's equipment. It's cold, damp, unfriendly."

"Magnetic absorbers in the walls to stop magnetic energy from killing the organisms outside. A coat of lead-based paint will keep the magnetism inside," Darius said.

"And?"

"A wooden table plus blocks - -"

"Why?"

"To check our manual dexterity. Machines to measure our endurance."

"And?"

Dahlia said, "There are some metal sheets where the repair shop was for them."

"Computers with keyboards to gauge our IQs," Darius went on.

"Judged by?"

"Our test scores."

"Who shall devise the tests?"

"They can be found on the Intermagnet, Wendy."

"The reason?"

"In the event of a magnetic crisis which has been expect ed by scientists like me."

"Suppose our insides are affected? We need an MRI."

"Too big for the basement," Walter objected.

"They manufacture portable ones, four to six feet tall. I know how to operate the machine having done brain scans."

"What would you be looking for?"

"Magnetized blood, oh dear. The Chihuahua, I have to have a new pet," Dahlia said.

"The machines' cost?"

"Plenty."

Dahlia raised her shoulders.

"When we're not being tested?"

"Hopefully, we rest."

"In?"

"Lounging chairs. We must be watched."

"How come?"

"We might display violent tendencies."

"We'd be watched from?"

"A control booth - - a module."

"What should we wear?"

"I recommend coveralls."

"Who will occupy the module?"

"I don't know yet."

"This should be considered an experiment?"

"Of course."

"The purpose?"

"To learn how high magnetism affects us and if we survive it."

"We could die?"

"The odds are too small to worry about."

"How will we be aware - - "

"A magnetometer will tell us. Walter will arrange the wiring."

#

He and Darius went to work, helped by the Eskimos (mostly Aleuts) who dug out the ground to extend the basement. Using cement blocks, they built a new wall. Then, with Plexiglas, they constructed a control booth, which resembled a huge transparent egg. The control room contained instruments for measuring magnetism, among others the wobbuloscope, also bought by Dahlia along with the egg and lounge chairs on the Internet; had them flown in ASAP along with the MRI by the pilot Gus who she talked to on the phone, despite the static. The wooden table and coveralls were purchased at the general store by Wendy. Trying on the coveralls, she danced, perhaps because she didn't want to reveal her fear.

Intermagnet showed photos on a Faraday chair and the Aleuts made it from tin they found in the ceiling of a torn-down shack.

The oilers had obtained several magnometers and Darius borrowed the device. Walter caused the number to flash on the screen.

EARTH ONE

"Meaning?" Dahlia asked.

"Simple," Darius said. "Normal magnetism but it might not stay put."

The handlers, as Darius referred to them, remained a problem.

"Who?" he asked.

"You decide," Dahlia said.

He deliberated and summoned Joe. "Have you a spouse?"

"Uh-huh. Josie."

"Would you help us?"

"What do I stand to gain?"

"Extra pay."

"Josie too?"

"O.K."

#

I took a week or so before Maglab was ready. During the interval the group watched a lot of TV.

Announcer: "Scientists now wonder if increased magnetism might be indirectly responsible for the increased sunlight that might account for skin cancer and blindness."

"Which gives our Maglab work special urgency," Darius remarked.

Would they be up to it? he asked himself. The experiment required serious challenges of strength, endurance and moral fortitude. Days might elapse before they emerged from their magnetic cocoon. Had they stockpiled sufficient food? Could Joe and Josie be trusted? How should they regard themselves? Laboratory rats that could be sacrificed for the greater good, the survival of mankind? (Wasn't that a bit pretentious? He hoped not.) Visualizing the dank basement, he inwardly cringed. When should they start? As soon as humanly possible.

#

Darius saw the portable toilets being lowered by Eskimo workers and thought: time to commence.

The group wore coveralls but it had been Dahlia's idea to dye what amounted to uniforms in different colors - - she had chosen carrot-red like her hair, a fashion statement; he supposed. Walter's choice was black to match his hair; Wendy picked gold, perhaps reflecting her hopes. He himself selected blue, the color of the sky on a clear day.

Red, black, gold, blue - - at least they'd be able to identify each other in the event any of them died.

Single file, they descended the narrow staircase - - carrot-red, black, gold, blue. All wore sneakers.

They padded to the rear of the basement where the control booth was, near the food and bottled water chutes and the work area with the wooden table. Close to that, the canvas lounge chairs for resting. Joe was already present; also a chubby woman who must be Josie, their eyes fixed on the computer screen for instructions, he assumed.

Walter had rigged the screen so that the group could read it.

RELAX!

DAHLIA

WENDY

WALTER

DARIUS

The computer rated them.

"First the wooden table," Josie said. She stood up in the control booth: short, bow-legged, unattractive.

"Put the blocks in the slots," Joe added.

"They're testing our manual dexterity," Darius said. "Timed, of course."

Each of them walked to the table and placed blocks in the slots.

WALTER

WENDY

DAHLIA

DARIUS

"What's being tested now?" Darius wondered.

"Must be coordination," Walter said. "And I'm the best."

"You're boasting as usual," Dahlia said.

"You expect me to be modest?" Walter said, lowering his black eyes.

"You'd be more attractive."

"I thought you found me attractive as I was."

"Well - - "

"I admire Walter because he's strong," Wendy said. "If he's humble too, well - - "

ALL YE WHO ENTER HERE ABANDON HOPE

"Who programmed that?" Walter asked.

"Me." Darius laughed. "I'm quoting Dante's <u>Inferno</u>."

Test Palindromes

"What the hell are those?" Dahlia questioned.

"Anything that reads the same backwards or forward," Darius explained. "The computer will provide examples."

ABLE WAS I ERE I SAW ELBA

"You touched nothing. The gadget must be interactive," Wendy said, staring at the screen.

"So it appears."

The group perched at desks, each equipped with a keyboard. The instruction read, "Type what you see."

18181

Dahlia typed

18181

She said, "Difficult? Negative."

ABLE WAS I ERE I SAW ELBA

Able was i ere i saw elba

"Easy."

"You were timed - - twenty seconds."

"Not long. Your turn, Darius."

It took him a minute to type the same words. "I'm a klutz," he admitted.

Walter needed almost a minute. "My fingers are too thick," he complained.

"I hate it when you feel sorry for yourself." Wendy said.

"If Walter turns into his opposite, you'd covet him."

Darius said, "And if I became arrogant, rude and uncaring, like him, you'd also covet me."

"I'll have to consider that," Wendy said. "While I'm capable."

"We must test your manual dexterity," Joe ordered.

Darius, at the table, tried to insert square pegs into round holes.

"We're also measuring IQs," Josie said. "Darius' ain't so hot. Next!"

Dahlia left the lounge chair and replaced Darius at the table.

"What do you see?"

"Triangular blocks that refuse to fit into round holes."

"Her IQ is down too," Joe observed.

On the wall a sign read

EARTH TWO

"Earths are a magnetic gauge," Darius informed the Aleuts. "Two earths are twice that of normal. Something is wrong. Check the magnetometer."

"Up," Joe reported.

Darius had the Intermagnet online. "The phenomenon must be local. Zero has occurred in other places."

"Is increased magnetism the reason Walter and you are opposing?" Dahlia asked.

"I'm certain their brains hemispheres have reversed." Wendy offered.

"Bullshit," Walter snarled, seemingly restored to his usual persona.

#

While Walter was on the portable toilet, Dahlia inquired, "How do you account for that?"

"Magnetism suddenly rose."

"Why?" Wendy said.

"A fluctuation that presages a turnaround. Magnetism will increase still more." He paused, "To be confirmed by Magsat."

"Magsat?"

"A NSA satellite that tracks terrestrial magnetism. It's in constant orbit. Also, the main magnetic field is modeled by the International

Reference Field (IGRF) and the World Magnetic Model (WMM). There are about two hundred magnetic observatories in the world."

"People must be worried."

"Only a handful of scientists are. People know nothing about magnetism. Now they shall."

"How do we learn what is observed?"

"The Intermagnet."

"You?"

"I just did."

"Mealtime," Josie muttered.

So as not to stop the tests, Walter had contrived a system by which food parcels were dropped periodically from the kitchen through tin chutes - - sandwiches, salads, bottles of water and milk. The group swallowed them slowly. Then the toilet break. When they resumed, the sign read

EARTH THREE

"Nothing to concern us - - yet," Darius told them. He examined the control booth. The Aleuts had vanished.

This wasn't a mystery. A plastic catheter through the wall went outside.

With little to do, Walter suggested a game of bridge with cards that would be used for the tests.

They pushed the chairs to the table. "Understand the rules?"

The others nodded so he riffled the cards like a pro and dealt.

Walter inspected his cards, "I win! A laydown."

"I remember," Dahlia said. "That's how you regard women. And you mostly win. But not with me."

"Tell with time," he said after a struggle.

"Walter is also guilty of backspeak," Darius noted.

The Eskimos returned, "Bad weather outside," Joe reported.

Josie said, "Dark clouds and flashes from the sky."

"Is your house equipped with lightning rods?" Joe asked.

"Didn't get to it," Dahlia said.

"We could have a fire," Wendy said.

"Let's try palindromes again" Josie said, ignoring her.

Dahlia typed, "…ere I saw elbow - -"

"Elba," Wendy corrected.

"My fingers jammed."

"Not your fingers. Your brain.

"Oh dear."

Then the computer presented new material.

IF I COULD TELL YOU I WOULD LET YOU NA

"That's from the poet Auden. Not <u>na</u> but know," Wendy said.

IT WAS THE BEST OF TIMES
IT WAS THE WORST OF TIMES

Dahlia typed

It was the bust of times.

It was the wurst of times

"Best not bust and worst, not wurst," Wendy mocked. ""You must be jealous and starved."

"I guess I am. Let's tea."

"Tea time? No. Eat, she means."

"I hate you, Wendy. You're always castigating me."

"And you deserve it," Wendy shouted.

They leaped from the lounge chairs, pummeling each other with fists.

"Violence isn't their styles," Darius pointed out.

"Yea, but it's getting w<u>u</u>rst," Walter rumbled.

"You sound like Dahlia," Darius said.

His mind's eye remained open. Through the "O" he saw.

Darius + Dahlia

Walter + Wendy

But likes repel. He'd have preferred opposites.

Darius + Dahlia

Walter + Wendy

However, for now, it wasn't to be.

Darius concentrated on the next test announced by Joe.

Visual Angular Resolution.

Designs floated on the computer screen. The job, he grasped, was to reconcile them into a coherent form. The triangles should become stars, he suspected, but he couldn't do it, though he tried.

The rest of them failed as well.

They must have lost IQ points and matters could get wurse - - no, worse.

EARTH SIX

The computerized sign told them.

Josie sneezed, announced a fifteen minute break and the group went upstairs where Darius checked the Intermagnet again. Alphonso, the calculus whiz, reported no changes in the terrestrial magnetic field had occurred, so the increase must be local - - in fact directly under the house. But, he feared, it would spread to the northern hemisphere and the southern one. The entire world would suffer disorientation like the dinos.

Meanwhile, the group would serve as litmus paper.

Would the litmus show blood? Would the group be reduced to murder? He gave a silent atheist's prayer they'd remain civilized.

Downstairs again, they resumed testing. All flunked Vary and Walter lost his temper, yelling at the Eskimos, "The tests are too fucking hard!"

"Not their fault," Darius advised.

"Of course it is. I could kill them. Come out of that shitty module and fight!"

Joe and Josie refused to emerge and Walter heaved wooden blocks at them. Safe behind the Plexiglas, they laughed, further infuriating him.

Walter told the group that, in addition to being a bridge champion, he'd excelled at wrestling. He challenged Joe to wrestle.

"No, but Josie will."

Walter gave up. However, Darius continued to fret about homicidal urges. Then he himself lost his temper with Dahlia over how to spell palindrome…two l's, she maintained…and he, a pacifist, attempted to strangle her. Fortunately, she proved more agile.

The last test of the day was announced by the Joe, a boxer. He dropped the improvised boxing gloves…canvas wrapped around chunks of cinderblocks from the module. "Darius vs. Walter" he said. "No excuses."

"I don't want to," Darius said. "Compared to me he's a giant."

"I'll fight with one hand behind my back," Walter thundered. He put on the gloves.

So did Darius. They squared off, Walter put his right hand behind his back and jabbed at Darius' nose.

"Unfair," Darius claimed. "He's a lefty."

"I am?" Walter replied and lowered his glove. "I'm confused."

Whereupon Darius bopped him in the nose.

Dahlia and Wendy giggled.

"I quit," Walter declared and patted Darius on the head.

#

That night, fearing hypermagnetism's pernicious effects, they slept in the basement where they could watch each other.

Toward dawn, Darius, always an early riser, spotted Wendy and Dahlia in the same sleeping bag. Wendy failed to shock him but Dahlia did.

She opened her eyes and whispered, "Blame the magnetism."

"Have fun?"

"Erus."

"Meaning sure?"

"Sey."

The Asian-American woman eyeballed him. "I didn't have nuf. I'm not reeuq now."

"Fun? Queer? You could have fooled me."

Walter snored.

Darius' homicidal urges subsided which indicated magnetism had too but for how long?

#

The next day, the tests started again. Their assignment: tying knots. All of them could tie square knots except Darius, clumsy as usual. He fared better with the hangman's noose.

"Who would you hang?" Wendy asked. "Walter?"

"Negative."

"Yourself?"

"Well - -" Should he commit suicide? Perhaps, rather than become a mental legume.

Dahlia seemed to read his mind. "You're not the suicidal sort."

"Suppose, just suppose, I am?"

However, that amounted to wishful thinking.

"Are you?"

He shook his head.

"I'm not either."

Wendy frowned and said, "I occasionally considered doing away with myself."

Wendy + Darius

He saw, then told them, "Maybe I <u>am</u> capable of suicide," a similar response to Wendy's. Likes repel.

Wendy + Darius = 0

Relieved, he mastered the square knot.

EARTH EIGHT

Magnetism was augmenting again and he experienced a renewed desire to kill Dahlia. He longed to put his hands around her fragile neck and choke her. But she remained too beautiful to die.

Wendy? Too intelligent. Who or what? He'd murder…no you didn't murder animals though PETA would define it that way…kill a dino except the creatures lived only in his fantasies. Yes, an end to fantasies. He'd be spared those dreadful visions.

But people would need visions to survive hypermagnetism. Maybe he'd discover a way out. Which told him the tests must continue.

Fatigued, the group clamored for dinner like angry swans. It arrived through the chutes when Joe pressed a button. They were completely dependent on the Aleuts.

Dissatisfied with water and milk, Walter demanded something stronger.

"Such as?" Dahlia said. "I know - - bourbon."

"O.K.," Walter muttered.

Could a drunken Walter cope with hypermagnetism? Darius asked himself.

Josie, empathizing with Walter, climbed upstairs and returned carrying a bottle of booze which Walter imbibed silently. At last he spoke.

"Fusb - -"

"Fusb?"

"Fuck – you – son – of – a – bitch. I invented an all-purpose cuss word."

"Aimed at whom?"

"The fusbing Aleuts who administered the tests."

"They didn't invent them," Darius said.

"So fusb those responsible," Walter fell asleep.

"Soon he'll snore," Wendy predicted.

"We must quit for the night," said Joe.

#

The next morning they heard the maddening whir of the drill.

"The oilers are here," Darius said excitedly. "I need to talk with them."

"The reason?"

"To learn how deep they've drilled, Dahlia. May I go upstairs?"

"Permission granted," Josie said. "You have fifteen minutes. The others must remain."

Darius raced to the front yard where he found the hardhats. "How far are you?"

"A coupla thousand feet."

"Got a reading on the magnetometer?"

"Up. Way up."

"Keep me posted."

Darius returned to the cellar.

"Good news?" Wendy wondered.

"No. Magnetism has increased."

"The tests must start again," Joe ordered.

"We'll flunk them," Darius warned. "Our IQ's will plummet."

As proved the case. The computer printed a map of the world. Instructed to show where Greenland was, Dahlia pointed at California. (The map contained shapes, not names.) Wendy placed San Francisco in the state of New York. Walter put Boston in the Baja Peninsula. Darius refused to take the test.

"I'm aware I'm mentally impaired."

"How?" Dahlia said.

"I don't remember what country we're in."

"Adanac," Dahlia replied.

"Canada," Wendy rebuked her.

"In the Southern Hemisphere," Walter maintained.

"The problem is our brain hemispheres don't provide correct information," Wendy explained.

"And yours?"

"The emas."

"Same?"

"Ko."

An emergency happened. Joe and Josie had to leave. The group went upstairs.

"When the magnetic crisis is finally finished, will you return to Chicago?" Wendy said to Dahlia.

"Haven't decided. If I do, I'm uncertain what career to pursue."

"Your choices?"

"People want me to enter politics. Young. A fresh face - -"

"And beautiful."

"- - run for city council."

Darius visualized Dahlia's campaign for city council – brisk, terse, sexy. He'd vote for her except he'd probably be dead.

"As?"

"A person who's against the politics of fear and stands for the common good. A Democrat, I think" Dahlia said.

"But - -"

"I know. I used to be a Republican. However, I've switched positions."

"Me too," Wendy said. "I was a radical…a Socialist…but I feel a kinship with the conservatives. I've reversed myself."

"As the magnetic poles might," Darius said, smiling faintly.

"Not humorous," Walter growled. "Whom do you take me for, a Republican?"

"Aren't you?" Dahlia asked.

"No. A dyed in the wool Democrat. A supporter of the common good."

"A kissing cousin!"

"You two are my opposite," Wendy declared.

Darius saw

$$Wendy + Walter$$

and perhaps

$$Wendy + Dahlia$$

Darius pondered. He could never be a Republican. No, now, a Democratic Socialist. Neutral, perhaps. Even a utopian. Or an observer, as always, lonely.

$$Darius + 0$$

"Let's watch TV," he said.

#

They watched commercials, one for sunblock.

SKIN

RECNAC

"Cancer. They've started spelling backwards in California," Dahlia pointed out.

USE SUNBLOCK X

"X for extra strength," Walter noted.

BUY

Pictures of toasters, brooms, vacuum cleaners, big cars, bottled water, hair and sex products, shoes, camping equipment, fishing rods, airplanes, greeting cards, foodstuffs, hotel rooms, mattresses, beach resorts, garbage bags, amusement parks, clothing, rubber tires, flowers, candy, heal balm, laxatives appeared.

"What we don't need more of," Wendy commented.

"Except for the sunblock," Darius said. "We can anticipate that the danger from UV radiation will move further north. We should send warnings."

"How?"

"Put them on You Tube."

Before they could, a buzzer instructed them to return downstairs.

Chapter Six

BACK IN THE CONTROL booth the Eskimos looked glum.
"What was the emergency?" Dahlia asked.

"Sun. Hotter than normal. A few of our relatives got sick."

"Heat exhaustion?"

"No. Skin turned red."

"Sunburn!"

"Us too. Smeared ourselves with seal oil but didn't help."

"It must be hazardous outside. We must remain in the house," Wendy cautioned.

"Not at night," Walter said.

"Night people!" Dahlia exclaimed.

"Let's watch TV," Darius again suggested.

Images of crowds and police cars at night.

Announcer: "Folks must stay indoors during the day…during the day. That's the new California law. Offenders will be penalized…penalized."

"For risking melanoma!" Wendy seemed shocked. "Skin cancer is supposed to be ones own responsibility."

"Fusb!" Darius shouted.

Announcer: "We have learned Canada is about to pass the same legislation."

"So the Aleuts won't be permitted to emerge in the sunlight either," Wendy noted.

"How will they fish?" Walter asked. "Or farm?"

"We'll starve," Dahlia said bitterly.

"Starvation, blindness, skin cancer - - bad ways to end." Darius observed.

"Blind, starving melanoma victims," Wendy muttered. "Couldn't be worse."

"Still, it could," Darius said. "Blind, skeletal melanoma victims with low IQs."

"We won't become stupid," Walter shouted. "That notion is parc. Crap, I wanted to say."

"But you didn't," Dahlia cried.

"In any case, the future looks bleak," Darius said.

"Even bleaker if a polar swap transpires."

Wendy rebuked him. "Transpires, if there is such a nomenclature, must refer to breathing. The proper word is happens. Will it?"

"Of course not," Walter said.

"I think the world can be boiled down to two types of people," Darius said, "skeptics and dogmatists of which Walter is a prime example. He sticks to his doctrine no matter what. The skeptic, though dubious, listens to evidence. I need to inspect the Intermagnet."

They climbed upstairs again and Alphonso Jones appeared on the computer.

He issued a warning to them. "Don't trust Alfred Nobel. He's a descendant of the Nobel who invented dynamite. This Nobel is a renegade scientist who intends to make a trillion dollars."

"How?" Darius asked.

"By selling credit default swaps short. He thinks the stock market will collapse when the polar reversal is inevitable."

"What is credit default?" Dahlia wondered.

"A seventy trillion dollar insurance business. He's flying to your area in a jet seaplane. Watch out!"

Darius stared at the group. "According to Jones, the Aurora Australis in the Southern Hemisphere has been spotted two months early. We can expect the same in the north."

"And then?"

"According to IGRF and WMM on the computer, the magnetic poles will take the shape of rings, expanding as they surround the earth until at the equator, they cross and proceed to opposite magnetic poles. Then north is south and vice versa."

"Permanently?"

"Until the next one, about a half-billion years hence."

"Will humans be around then?"

"Will homo-sapiens survive? Can we adapt? Depends."

"On?"

"Our ability to transcend, during the swap, the loss of the sense of direction and insanity."

"What kind?"

"Bipolar disorder, symptomized by extreme mood swings."

"Leading to?"

"Mass homicides."

"Kcuf," Walter exploded. "Excuse me, fuck!"

"Homicide, for us, would be out of character, wouldn't it?" Wendy said.

"Who knows?" Darius said. "We haven't been tested for that."

"Here's the chance," Walter said. "I could kill our handlers."

"Why?"

"The darkness, the boredom of our routine, the monotony of existence but most of all their lousy cuisine."

The group went back to the basement. The engineer examined the module and its Plexiglas windows. "A tough nut to crack if they resist."

"Resist?"

"They will assume we're hostile."

"We?"

""You'll help, of course. You feel resentment too, don't you?"

"Sure. We'll need a plan. Dahlia, pretend to be sick. When Joe comes out of the control booth, I'll clobber him."

"My role?" Wendy said.

"You're a medical doctor. Tell them she can't be helped down here."

"O.K."

"I refuse to participate," Darius said.

"The reason?"

"I don't believe in violence."

"As a Christian I don't either - -" Dahlia stepped before the module. She moaned "I'm ill."

"What's the matter?" Josie said.

"I have a pain in my chest."

"She's faking," Joe warned Josie.

"My heart throbs too fast."

"Magnetism couldn't cause that," was Josie's opinion.

"I had rheumatic fever as a child," Dahlia pleaded.

"She's a liar," Joe claimed.

Now the hard part, Darius thought. He watched Dahlia close her eyes, clutch her chest, breathe fast and sink gently to the floor. The tremulous sigh, she had to hope, sounded like a dying person.

"But - -" Joe wavered.

"Take her pulse, doctor," Josie said.

Wendy sobbed but remained in place.

"Gertz!"

Walter acted deaf.

"Sykes!"

Darius sat on his hands.

"What to do?" Joe said.

"Let her die," Josie said wearily.

"We'd better make sure she's perished," Joe said.

"I pray she hasn't. We'd have to dispose of the body."

"I should inspect the corpse," Joe said and jumped out of the module.

Walter, waiting, pounced.

"What - -"

"I'm going to hurt you."

"The reason?"

"You've been mistreating us."

"But the tests were your idea!"

"They didn't need to be so unpleasant."

Joe shrugged.

Bow-legged and plump, Josie emerged from the control booth, spittle on her lips. "I wanna fight!"

""Not with me," Walter said, "Dahlia?"

"I abjure physical combat," said the svelte woman.

"Wendy?"

"I'd rather dance with her."

"Cowards," Josie screamed. "We quit." She and Joe departed in a huff.

PART TWO

Chapter Seven

"Now what?" Dahlia said.

"Either we vegetate or we continue the tests in preparation for the magnetic emergency."

"The latter is the obvious choice," Wendy said. "But how do we get the handlers back?"

"More money?" Dahlia said.

"O.K., " Walter agreed. "But first we have to find them."

Upstairs, they searched for Joe and Josie with no results.

"Let's look outside," Dahlia said.

But they saw nothing.

Walter suggested the saloon and in the Humvee they went there. Josie perched at the table, nursing a beer.

"Joe?" Dahlia asked.

"Gone fishin'."

"We need you in Maglab," Darius said.

"Won't go. You tried to kill us."

"Would you return?"

"Naw. Too dangerous."

"We won't attack you again," Wendy promised.

"I don't believe you."

"Suppose we sweeten the deal?" Dahlia said.

"Huh?"

"Offer more dough."

"Can't decide."

"What if I told you a disaster would be avoided with your help?" Darius said.

"Disaster? Describe it."

"Let's just say the world would be turned upside down."

"Explain, dammit."

"We'd be fucked up."

"Oh. How?"

"Sunburns could get worse."

"O.K. To the basement again."

EARTH TEN

The next test required a rowing machine and Walter instructed the Eskimos on how to build it.

"I was an oarsman at MIT," he gold the group. "And we always won."

"As with everything else," Dahlia remarked sarcastically.

The Eskimos assembled the machine from stuff they found on the beach - - an old rowboat, a pair of barnacle-encrusted oars which they cleaned, and an oven timer. Unnoticed by the group, they inserted powerful magnets in the oarlocks.

These magnets had been part of the stuff Dahlia had bought in Chicago, on orders of Darius. He had studied the procedures on the Intermagnet.

Joe read aloud the brief instructions.

"One. You will get on board the boat, grip the oars and row. You will be timed."

"Two. You will cross your hands and row. You will be timed."

"Three. As you encounter resistance, you will continue rowing. The timer remains on."

"Sounds simple," Walter said. He asked the control booth, "Who's first?"

"Might as well be you," Joe said.

The rowing machine stood in the center of the chamber, supported by concrete blocks. Walter climbed in and seized the oars, rowing and smiling.

"Cross you hands," Joe commanded.

Walter complied.

"Any problems?"

Walter rowing empty air was a ludicrous spectacle, so they laughed.

Josie used a stop watch. "Time satisfactory."

The others received a similar score.

#

The tests went on for an hour and their scores began to slip.

The sign flashed.

EARTH FIFTEEN

"It will get harder," Darius predicted. "Magnetism is augmenting."

And so were the magnets.

Walter pulled harder on the oars but the results proved unsatisfactory.

Joe said, "Cross you hands."

Walter tried but his left hand landed on his right. The others fared no better.

"A polar swap is nigh," Darius concluded.

"What's the next test?" Dahlia asked.

"Word puzzles," Joe answered. "We'll pause until you take the machine apart."

#

"How much longer will we be trapped down here?" Wendy wanted to know.

"Maybe it's worth the agony if we learn how to cope with hypermagnetism," Darius said.

"Including the loss of our sense of direction?"

"I assume. The Intermagnet wizards must have thought of that."

"Who are they?"

"Scientists, as I told you. They try to anticipate emergencies."

"As bad as this one portends?"

"Well - -"

The buzzer signaled the tests. Instead of the rowing machine was the table on which jumbled pile of cardboard pieces lay. "Put them together," Joe said, tone peremptory.

Dahlia tried first and found few matches. She uttered a frustrated scream "That's all I can accomplish."

Walter followed. "I suspect it's a map."

Wendy, expanding the puzzle, nodded. "The northern hemisphere! But we've already played the game."

"It's not simply a game," Darius insisted. "I'm convinced this is a map of the Arctic region."

Dahlia scurried to the opposite end of the table, quickly matching pieces. "Antarctica," she declared. "And there's the South Pole."

"Must be the magnetic South Pole," Darius said. "They're not quite identical. The same with the North. But what's that?" He assembled more pieces. "The North Pole appears to have moved south."

"And with the south, versa-vice," Dahlia reported.

"Vice-versa?" Wendy queried.

"Dahlia's wordslip is another indication the situation is serious," said Darius. He fit together still more pieces. "We've solved the puzzle. It depicts a polar swap."

"But pieces remain," Walter said.

"Not a mystery. The collapse of the earth's magnetic system might lead to as many as eight magnetic poles, also termed dipoles," as I said. "They move."

"In which direction would the compass point"

"Everywhere."

"The result?"

"Complete chaos. But at least we've solved the puzzle."

Chaos. The inevitable outcome Darius had predicted.

"You deserve a reward," Josie said.

"For?"

"Finding a solution." If only he had. "Take the night off."

The group mounted the stairs. Except for Darius, they were in a festive mood.

"What are we celebrating?" Dahlia said. "We're supposed to have fun."

"How?" Dahlia wondered.

"An orgy?" Walter suggested. "Negative. You're too conventional. Break out the drinks."

Not many drinks later, the quarrels commenced.

"Which way were the poles heading?" Dahlia asked Wendy.

"A trick question. North to south and the opposite."

"Wrong. East to west and the opposite."

"You're both correct because of the dipoles."

"Do dipoles have opposites?"

Darius thought, everything has its opposite: likes repel while opposites attract. He saw in his mind's eye

Wendy + Walter

Dahlia + Darius

Then Dahlia's snide remark infuriated him. "Rum and you are a bad combination, as I pointed out."

Bad.

`His vision changed: Darius + Wendy.

But Wendy said, "When drunk, Darius is unappealing."

Wendy + Darius = 0

He felt a murderous rage.

Whom would he kill?

He'd get to that afterwards.

Chaos.

#

Darius remembered the heat death, a concept of physicists, which described the universe in terms of forms. When heat grew excessive, the forms dissolved, leaving chaos, and, because of magnetism the van Allen belts offered less protection from solar radiation. The result, record heat in the Arctic region.

Even in northwestern Canada it was steaming hot. The house lacked air-conditioning so the group Humveed to the litter-strewn beach.

"Too cold to swim," Dahlia said, testing the water with a tentative finger.

"I'm a good swimmer, but the wind is rising," Wendy observed.

"And getting stronger, like a mini-hurricane. Why?" Walter asked.

"The solar radiation may be creating a vacuum that the wind fills," Darius offered. "Another example of the danger facing the world."

"Gale force winds, devastating heat, skin cancer, blindness, disorientation - -omigod," Dahlia shrieked. "Depressing."

"We must look on the bright side but where?" Wendy lamented.

Clouds filled the sky, blocking the dreadful sun, and it felt cooler. "Perhaps nature is our only hope," Darius mused. He glimpsed in his mind's eye

LIKES REPEL

Perhaps a solution for the magnetic emergency that gripped the world, perhaps a description of the current state of affairs between Dahlia and him.

He said to her, "I'd be content were we opposites."

"Grow two heads," she retorted.

"You're sarcastic."

"Unlike you."

"Doesn't that render us opposites?"

"Well - -"

"If so, under the laws of magnetism, we're attracted to each other."

"What about our emotions? Surely they count."

"Of course. But magnetic mischief, though subtle, is potent."

"More than free will?"

"Possibly. I don't know. Depends on what happens."

"To?"

"Us."

"Meaning?"

"Whether we retain our sanity."

#

Having sobered up, the group returned to the house where they snacked and went to bed.

Perhaps he'd retired too early but Darius woke in the middle of the night, he assumed. His watch, which had metal parts, had stopped. He turned on the light over his bed. In the picture a sailboat seemed to move! If a magnetic surge had occurred, this was the most dangerous time.

Once more, in his mind's eye, he saw"

Darius Sykes, clad in coveralls, prowls the second floor, lips curled down. He clutches a wooden mallet and opens Wendy's door. She lies on her back, dark hair wreathing the pillow. Her smile hints she's dreaming. About? Him, he hopes. He wants to kiss her but fears she'll wake. Suddenly her slanted eyelids flutter and she sighs. He needn't have worried - - she's fast asleep, hands folded across her breasts. He may love her but she must perish. Why? He doesn't know, maybe never shall. He raises the mallet but hesitates. Is he having doubts? No. he's afraid he'll wretch. He pounds her skull and blood spatters the coveralls - -

Darius heads downstairs. Which way to go? In the kitchen, having abandoned the mallet he seizes a cleaver and moves right. He hears snores from Walter's bedroom and opens the door. The snoring ceases. Walter is always on guard. Darius creeps nearer and Walter turns on his back, exposing his throat. Before Darius can strike, Walter opens his oculars. Does he spot Darius? No. the eyes close again. Is the moment propitious? Yes, except the restless Walter rolls on his side, muscular arms over his throat. Perhaps he subconsciously suspects he's entered the danger zone. And he moans but then smiles. Walter must be dreaming. Probably of Dahlia. Darius' resolve strengthens. Murdering Walter will amount to a sort of ecstasy so Darius attacks Walter's neck.

Next, he scurries to Dahlia's room. Though sleeping, she frowns. He has left the cleaver on Walter's bed; his hands are empty like his soul. Will he miss Dahlia? Yes, but she's better off dead than unobtainable. How shall he kill her? Strangulation? Too obvious. And why does she frown? She must be dreaming of him. He needs a novel method. Which? While he considers, Dahlia pushes the straps of her nightgown aside, exposing her breasts, and burps. She's imbibed excessively. For that, he's grateful. She'll never be aware what killed her. He must decide how. Asphyxiation? She deserves it because she's too loquacious. Darius rips off a piece of her nightgown and packs her mouth. Dahlia shudders, then dies.

Still in his mind's eye, Darius sees Wendy dodging the mallet and rising. He imagines her cerebrations.

Darius is stupid in trying to kill me. For one thing, I'm too smart. For another, I'm sexier than Dahlia. He ought to be attracted to me. I'm assuming he'll menace her as well. And maybe Walter whom Darius is jealous of. He (Darius) must be bonkers. Perhaps we all are. Given the chance, I'll try to kill Darius. How? I could use help. I wonder if Walter will agree.

Darius visualizes Walter and almost hears his thoughts.

For attempting to murder me while I slept, Darius is a coward. He wouldn't have dared had I been awake. He's furious since both Dahlia and Wendy prefer me. And they show good judgment since I'm less alarmist besides being more handsome which must be obvious even to him. I'll seek revenge, yes. I'll deprive Darius of what he values most - - I'll beat his brains out. I anticipate Wendy's and Dahlia's cooperation.

Dahlia considers Walter's plan. She has chewed and swallowed the cloth and remains alert. I wish to help Walter and Wendy. I don't want revenge; pity is what I feel. Darius is in a weak mental state, but that's a poor excuse. He must be killed.

The three converge at Darius' bedroom where he has sought refuge. Wendy hold a mallet, Walter a cleaver, Dahlia a strip of cloth. They - -

Darius had been dreaming. But that might be a harbinger of things to come.

#

The buzzer summoned them to Maglab where Joe and Josie waited.

"Have a good night?" she asked.

"Negative," they replied in unison.

"What seems to be the problem?"

"Don't ask," Walter said and groaned.

"Let's tell them," Wendy pleaded.

"Yes," Dahlia echoed.

"The truth is - -" Darius pointed

EARTH 20

"We've lost our marbles."

"A stupid remark," Wendy said.

"Cowardly," Walter added.

"I pity him," Dahlia said.

"Here we go again," Darius said. Not for the first time, he thought.

"The tests," Joe said.

Before they could begin, a loud noise sounded outside. Josie raced on her bow legs upstairs and quickly returned.

"The oil guys." She motioned toward Darius. "The fellas need to talk with you."

The group traipsed after Darius. In the front yard, they met the oilers. "Anything new?" he asked.

"We're drilling hard but have forgotten how to read the doohickey."

"Doohickey? Gizmo? Gadget? Magnometer?"

"Yeah."

"It has numbers printed on the dial."

"We can't count now."

"Mentally, they're downhill," Darius observed.

"That's true of us, isn't it?" Wendy questioned. "Haven't we entered the zone of danger?"

"What's that?" Dahlia wished to know.

"A French sociologist...I forget his name. Oh yes, Durkheim, Emile Durkheim...postulated that we willingly enter the danger zone where death waits. If such weren't the case with us, we wouldn't be here."

"You make us sound almost suicidal."

"In a way - -"

"At least we can add and subtract," Walter exalted.

"But for how long" Darius wondered.

The tests continued for the remainder of the day, yielding mediocre results.

"We'll give you the night off for so-so scores," a handler said. "Maybe you need a break."

#

In a dour mood, the group went to the Humvee. It was Darius who suggested a visit to the tavern.

"You?" Walter said.

"I think we require cheering up."

They Humveed to the saloon whose name had changed to NSE. "There's a compass embedded in the sign," an Aleut confided.

"The north magnetic pole must be shifting further south."

"We've seen ice floes and a polar bear in Resolute Bay."

"Are you cheered up?" sarcastic Dahlia said.

"No. The world's about to be reversed."

"And us. Our emotions will point in the opposite direction," Wendy advised. "That shall be true everywhere."

"Couples are bound to split," Walter said. "I envy divorce lawyers who'll be getting rich."

"You ignore politics," Darius cautioned. "Voters might elect extremists who would confiscate wealth though not mine."

"Socialists? Communists?"

"And perhaps the world is likely to become more polarized."

"What about the Muslims?"

"I don't know. Osama bin Laden will decide."

"In any case," Wendy said, "the important thing is polarization."

"I concur," Darius said. "People would be moving in many directions. Anarchy could result."

"And crime," Walter declared. "It might become rampant."

In his mind's eye Darius saw: police choppers over crowded streets, black men clashing with whites, books about the new Dark Age, teen girls sporting shaved heads and pierced ears masturbating on church steps, armed robberies, dead cops, marijuana growing in city parks, bombs exploding in supermarkets, TV stations on fire, Hollywood spelled backwards, doowylloH, peaceful parades becoming mob scenes, widespread arson, cliterectomy and torture among Americans, plus numberless acts of domestic violence.

"It will be out of control," Darius said. "And we can do nothing."

"Or make matters worse with your impossible predictions," Walter said.

"This isn't cheering me," Darius muttered and stalked out.

"He worries me," Dahlia said.

"Is he manic depressive?" Wendy asked. "Could he commit suicide?"

"We must watch him carefully," Walter advised.

#

The next test involved a stationary bicycle. "All you need to do is peddle," Joe announced.

"Sounds easy," Darius said.

"Timer's set."

After Darius had pedaled awhile, Joe said, "Not bad. Ten m.p.h., except your pedaling in reverse."

"I am?"

"Sure."

Had not the others flunked, Darius would have been sad. As it was, he tried to forget.

"Where am I?"

"You don't remember?"

"Not a thing."

"Your name?"

"What am I called, you mean? I don't know."

"Have you no memory at all?"

"Only sometimes."

"Suffer from amnesia?"

"I lack a logical answer. Amnesia would prevent me from recalling. I only know I'm alive because I'm not dead."

"Dead?"

"When I'm not alive."

"But he failed the bicycle test."

"Isn't it possible the spokes were magnetized?" Wendy asked.

"I don't know, but it's too painful for him to remember," was Dahlia's opinion.

"Right," Wendy agreed. "In any case, he isn't an amnesiac. What do you think, Walter?"

"I forget," Walter said.

Darius seemed alert. "Neither suicide or amnesia will prevent a polar swap." He looked at the sign which read

EARTH TWENTY-FIVE

In the module, Josie studied the instructions and the wobbuloscope. She said, "From now on no metal objects are permitted in Maglab. No keys, no coins (except copper pennies) or various pieces of ferrous metal. Otherwise, you might be guilty of murder."

Walter elaborated. "Flying ferrous objects like watches might decapitate a person."

"But - -" Dahlia started to say.

"I realize it's closer to negligence than homicide."

"But what are objects attracted to?"

Darius explained, "The magnetic field." He pointed at the sign, "Everything metal except tin will be magnetized."

"Outside Maglab?"

"No. Soon enough, however."

"Walter," asked Wendy, "could you install a video gadget that would give us Magsat's reading of the situation?"

"I'll try," the electrical engineer said.

#

Maglab was separated from the rest of the basement by a partition. Behind it Walter found in the workshop an old TV set which he took apart, attaching the screen to a long piece of wire he ran from the roof. A V-shaped metal bar would serve for an aerial.

On the Intermagnet, Darius learned when the magnetic satellite would traverse the Arctic region. By aiming the aerial at the right patch of sky at the right time, with luck, he ought to receive the signal.

Their luck held. The Maglab screen showed the true North Pole oozing yellow.

"What's that?" asked Josie. The handlers hadn't been told the purpose of Walter's activities.

"You're looking at disaster," Darius said.

"How soon?"

Darius frowned.

#

Walter remained skeptical but said, that night, "We need a short-wave radio and an electronic compass."

"Why?" Dahlia asked.

"In the unlikely event Darius is correct, we must have a way of what's happening here and in the world."

"The general store must have the radio. I'm sure they don't carry electronic compasses."

"To obtain the accuracy of an electronic compass, a mechanical one would have to be very long."

"Build it in the backyard," Dahlia said.

Walter's compass consisted of a slender, ten-foot metal needle suspended on a cement block over a shallow pit about twenty feet in circumference inscribed with dozens of marks.

"You constructed a gadget alone?"

"Aleuts helped."

"What are the marks?"

"They represent degrees inside the compass points. Were we positioned at the north magnetic pole the needle would dip until it stands vertical. As it is, if the needle shifts only minutely we'll know at once even during a Magsat malfunction."

"A sort of fail-safe procedure?"

"We've covered all the bases, not that we had to."

"You're hard to convince, Walter." Darius said. "The yellow ooze?"

Walter farted. "An optical illusion?"

"Negative. Let's purchase the radio."

#

Back at the general store, having selected a short-wave radio over satellite radio because short-wave was more dependable and free, Darius asked the Eskimo clerk, "The price?"

"U.S. or Canadian dollars?"

"Which for me would be cheaper?"

"U.S. dollars."

"The buck used to be worth a lot more than the Canadian one."

"The U.S. dollar was just devalued because people don't want to live there."

"The reason?"

"Many. The heat. Skin cancer - -"

"A pandemic?"

"Is that the word? Yes."

Darius said to Walter," It's not only California now."

#

Walter, having charged the radio to Dahlia's account, the group returned to the house where he ran a wire up a chimney and said, "The equipment?"

Darius gestured at an empty table on which he placed the transmitter and receiver. "I'll give it a whirl."

"Don't you need an ID number?"

He checked the box. "Has one already. WRES. Stands for Resolute."

Walter plugged in the radio and the group listened.

"Hello, WRES…Hi, WRES."

"Nothing of consequence seems to have happened."

"Nor here," Darius said.

Wendy remarked, "We should inspect the compass."

They went outside. Walter looked and growled, "The needle has deviated fractionally."

"Is that significant?"

Walter shook his head but Darius shouted. "It might be the beginning." "Of?"

He refused to respond.

Yawning, Dahlia said, "Let's watch TV."

#

In the house again, she clicked on the TV.

Announcer: "Traffic accidents, according to AAA, have increased markedly from coast to coast, coast to coast. Drivers, drivers, don't seem capable of staying in lanes. (Images of vehicular accidents.) They swerve, try to find an opening, then crash. Some have complained of dizziness - -"

Darius commented, "Disequilibrium. The first sign, I suppose, of a magnetic crisis."

"- - others insisted their vision has been impaired by the blinding sun."

"Let them get dark glasses," Walter said grumpily.

"The van Allen belts," Darius repeated. "You won't accept the gravity of the situation."

"But I will. I just don't think it's as bad as you think."

"Can I persuade you?"

"Negative, I'll rely on the compass."

He checked outside, and returned, "Hasn't budged."

"It will," Darius predicted.

"When?"

"Any time now."

"O.K." Dahlia said and they gathered around the long table in the livingroom. Walter poured a slug of bourbon and gulped it. "Cheers!"

"I'll take bourbon too," Dahlia said, licking her lips.

"I'll have vodka instead of my usual sake," Wendy said. "Darius?"

He hesitated. Soda or rum? What the hell. He'd risk intoxication.

A few drinks later the quarrels commenced.

"Which way were the poles heading?" Dahlia asked Wendy.

"North to south and the opposite."

"Wrong! East to west and the opposite."

Darius sighed, "You're both correct because of the dipoles."

"Their opposite is - -"

Darius thought: it's all a matter of opposites which repel while likes attract. He saw in his mind's eye

Wendy + Walter

Dahlia + Darius

Then Dahlia's snide remark infuriated him. "Rum and you are a bad combination."

His vision changed

Darius + Wendy

But Wendy said, "When drunk, Darius is unappealing."

"Is there time before dinner?" Dahlia said and smiled.

"If we hurry." Darius returned the smile.

"So it might be weeks?"

"Or days."

But Walter suddenly reversed positions. "Now!"

"Bullshit!" Darius shouted.

"I'd describe this as a magnetic flux," Wendy declared. "You change your minds. You can't distinguish between untruth and truth."

"She might be right," Walter said.

"Who knows?" Darius said. "It seems to me half-truths prevail in our society."

"During a polar swap everyone will prevaricate," Dahlia said.

"Lie? Yes," Wendy said. "It will be a strange new world."

"Maybe we should go home," Dahlia said.

Announcer: "Flights have been cancelled - - "

"So much for that," Darius said. "We're trapped here."

"Temporarily," Walter said. "The compass might reverse."

"Yeah," Wendy mouthed.

Opposites attract, Darius reminded himself and saw in his mind's eye

Darius + Wendy

Dahlia said, "I can rent a private jet."

Dahlia + Walter

They heard the oilers cheer.

"Must have struck oil." Walter said.

"I have even more money now." Dahlia laughed.

"Money won't count in tomorrow's world," Darius said. "Everyone will be reduced to poverty."

"Except the oil traders," Walter objected.

"Them too if nobody can afford to drive."

"What about cars?"

"A thing of the past. A relic. We'd have to revert to carts pulled by horses and oxen."

"Slow but reliable," Wendy said.

"The animals would become blind as well except for mice, raccoons and other nocturnal animals. Not a pretty picture - - blind animals pulling blind humans."

"You're a pessimist, Darius." Walter said.

"Dyed in the wool now," Darius mocked. "But realistic."

"We'll see." Walter said.

"If we can."

#

On the Intermagnet they learned a Command Center, part of the National Institute of Health and Prevention had been organized in Washington, D.C. It dispatched frequent bulletins.

One announced, "The magnetic crisis has become worldwide. Compasses all over the globe are malfunctioning. What's north and what's south is no longer clear. The same applies to east and west. On a light note, Civil War buffs want the Confederates declared the victor."

The next blog said, "The global oil supply has risen, according to recent estimates but are we wise to use it? The temperature is up everywhere - -"

"What about my petroleum stocks?" Dahlia caviled.

"Down, I bet," Walter said.

" - - we need cooler energy. As for nuclear power, we don't know how to dispose of the waste."

"A double bind," Wendy observed. "Nothing left but coal."

"You're forgetting a number of things…windmills, for instance… and, most important, geothermal energy," Walter reminded.

"But," Darius said, "you're ignoring that, as the earth's inner core changes speed, too much heat will be produced. Geothermal energy might be hazardous."

"Is there cold energy?" Dahlia wondered.

"If so, it must be from outer space and beyond our reach. A hopeless situation."

The subsequent bulletin stated, "Only a revolution can save us."

"By whom," Dahlia asked. "The far left or right extremists?"

"The center can not hold," Darius said, "I'm quoting, the poet Yeats."

"In a pinch I'd choose the righties," Walter said.

"I'm a leftist until I die," Wendy proclaimed. "Dahlia?"

She looked at Darius. "Well - -"

The Command Center blogs stopped.

Chapter Eight

"Now what?" Wendy asked.

"We wait," Darius said.

"For?"

"I wish I understood. The end, perhaps."

"Negative. We must continue the tests. Where are Joe and Josie? We ought to find them."

Josie said Joe was out fishing and should be back soon. The group hastened to the dock. At last the sloop appeared through the haze.

Joe climbed down. "Bad trip," he said. "I caught - - " He held up a two-headed salmon.

"A monstrosity," Dahlia yelped.

"It should go on the wall," Walter said.

"Is magnetism affecting evolution?" Darius asked.

"Is that why you were late?" Wendy inquired.

"Partly," Joe replied. "The other reason was the tide flowed in the wrong direction."

They went into the tavern whose name now read NNE.

The mutant salmon was about a foot long. Joe chopped off the upper half and put the portion in vodka.

"Formaldehyde would be better but vodka will do," Wendy said.

Joe mounted the salmon heads on a plaque and nailed it to the wall. At the same moment, the preacher arrived.

"Jeremy!" the Aleuts shouted.

He looked at the fish, cried "Satan created this!" stared in every direction and fled.

Others sank to their knees, wailing or pounded on the tables which, Darius noticed, had N   inscribed. The compass might have shifted in modern times. A warning scientists had ignored.

Darius didn't seem disturbed. "I'd describe the bi-headed fish as devolution. It must swim slower than its rivals and find less to eat, a disadvantage."

"Might there be two-headed whales?"

Darius shrugged.

"How would you characterize the creature in human terms?" Dahlia asked.

"A freak with a minimal chance to survive."

"How did the fish come into being?"

"Perhaps hypermagnetism affected its genes."

True? I don't know but I'm compelled to present an answer. The same with the tide.

"Was the reverse tide Joe encountered related to a polar swap?"

"Maybe."

Glib? Sure but I must convince them I <u>know</u> a reversal is at hand.

The group Humveed to the house. Walter checked the compass which had barely budged. Magsat showed nothing new. <u>The calm before the storm.</u>

But the Command Center blogs started again. They warned of a major magnetic episode.

EARTH THIRTY-FIVE

Darius gestured at the sign. "See?"

"It's like he's saying 'I told you so'," Wendy commented.

They sat doing nothing until at last Joe and Josie returned. "The next test concerns sex." Josie said.

"Xes?" Dahlia asked.

"Sex," Joe said distinctly.

"You mean redneg?"

"Huh?"

"Gender," Darius declared.

"Is there a difference?"

"I'm sure there is. Now the test. As usual, you will be timed. Dahlia, mount the table."

Dahlia did.

"Spread your legs."

Dahlia opened her legs.

"Kiss your lover."

Dahlia wiggled her toes.

"Have sex with him."

Dahlia displayed a fist.

"That's more like boxing," Josie noted.

Without warning, a tin object shaped like an envelope swung from a niche in the wall. At the same moment the magnetism increased. "The Faraday cage," Darius said. "It's supposed to protect us."

"From?" Dahlia said.

"Leukemia, I suppose."

"But there's only room for one of us," Wendy complained, "Who?"

"I'm too big to fit," Walter said.

"I hate being confined," Dahlia said.

"Reminds me of a hospital bed. I refuse." Wendy added. "Darius?"

"I don't want to survive without you."

"This test is null and void," Joe declared.

"At least we needn't worry about two-headed kids," Darius said.

But I'm not really optimistic. The liverwurst…worst…might happen, probably shall. Kcuf! I might become my opposite, an ignorant thug. A polar swap will hasten our decline, already happening as we grow more stupid. Why? A misguided sense of power, I suppose, plus a lack of pathos. How American! Arrogant! A polar swap will teach us humility <u>if</u> we live.

Walter was saying, "You look sad, Darius. What were you thinking of?"

"What the world would be like minus us. In the same fashion mammals replaced the dinos. By? Don't ask me."

"Imagine it or them."

"A new bread of homosapien. Homsapiensapien. Or Sapein-Sapien. Eons might elapse before a new race evolves - - a gentler, more tranquil folk."

"If not?"

"Then mankind - - "

"Don't forget women," Dahlia interrupted.

"- - will be remembered as raffish and bellicose."

"Why?"

Darius failed to answer.

"Perhaps a polar turnaround is our only hope," Wendy said.

" Not us. <u>Them</u>."

Darius sat, resembling a weary Buddha, in contemplation. But just for a while. Soon, he remarked, "Walter, check the radio."

Walter went to the kitchen, the others behind. He switched on the short-wave radio and they heard, despite the static, several reports from hams.

"Hello, This is Canberra - -"

"Where is that?" Wendy asked.

"Australia, of course."

"Don't condescend."

"We have witnessed UFOs. It's too early for the Southern Lights - -"

Fade out.

"What happened?" Dahlia said.

"Something awful? We'll never know."

"Unless we suffer the same fate," Wendy said.

"I wonder if the needle has shifted," Walter said.

Darius sighed and Walter switched stations. "Bangor, Maine here. I own a lobster farm but the water has turned so hot the critters are cooking in their pens, I'll go bankrupt - - "

"We can't expect the same standard of living p.p.s." Darius said.

"P.p.s.?" Walter inquired.

"Post polar swap."

"After the event, he means," Dahlia said, "Why, Darius?"

"Because the economy will suffer. Vastly increased sunlight will wither crops. No clouds will lead to a drought further diminishing farm products. Food prices will rise, "call it magflection." Contributing to rampant inflation, bringing a decrease in the sale of factory goods. Unemployment must rise as the result."

"Is that all?"

"Negative. People won't be able to pay their mortgages…mort, in other words death…and foreclosures must increase, especially since the terms were intended to put them in default. Millions of displaced people seeking shelter in addition to those hoping to avoid skin cancer and blindness. A bleak picture."

"What are my prospects?" Dahlia asked.

"You've always been rich. Maybe less so in the future?"

"This is Dallas. The sky has turned a weird shade of yellow. Is it a dust storm? Bizarre - -"

"The world will be bizarre," Darius predicted.

"Strange?" Wendy said. "In what sense?"

"Nothing would make sense. Truths would be untruths, untruths true."

"Liars mistaken for truth-tellers?"

"And the opposite."

"A sort of anti-world."

"Exactly."

"How would I survive in such a world?" Dahlia cried.

"Poor and, without you, lonely," Darius said.

"Marry an Aleut," Walter joked. "And live in the Aleutian Islands."

"I'd be jealous," said Darius.

"Me too," Wendy said.

"How can I believe that? A true untruth!"

"A half-truth then. Half of me loves you."

"Which half?"

"The Jewish portion," Walter said. "From the waist down."

"Is that enough?"

"Better to accept what you've got."

"Which is zero now."

A scratchy voice said on the radio, "I'm alone in hell - -" The voice faded out. "- - the Florida panhandle. I've been stung by a bunch of bees and I'm swelling up. I live in a wilderness. I gave the cops my coordinates but they don't seem able to find me." Static followed by silence.

"He must be dead. Anaphylactic shock," Wendy diagnosed.

"Magnetism explains why they failed to find him," Darius said.

The magnetic phenomenon is moving north," Walter said, "even though I only half believe in it."

"Is the glass half full or half empty?"

"Empty."

"He's a pessimist," Dahlia decided.

"Maybe poptimist would be a better word," Darius declared.

"That defines you?" Dahlia asked.

"I suppose."

"Not me. I'm an optimist."

"We're sort of opposites."

Darius + Dahlia = ½

he saw. Was that sufficient?

From the radio a voice boomed, "I'm in eastern Long Island, New York. We've seen yellow clouds but they've dissipated. I expect the sky will clear."

"A total optimist," Darius said. "He hasn't encountered hypermagnetism yet."

"In any case it's moving south," Wendy said.

A message from Russia arrived. "Moscow here, Is anyone listening? I've labored to master English. Respond, please."

"We can hear but lack the power to transmit," Walter said.

"My compass is going crazy - -"

"Hypermagnetism must be global now," Darius observed.

"I'm hearing loud noises in my head. Help - -"

#

They trouped to the yard. The needle dipped and had changed by "several degrees of arc", Walter explained, not much but enough to presage a magnetic event, Darius said. And what occurred here would also occur in the southern half of the globe, according to him.

Back inside the house, he inspected the computer for blogs from the Command Center. One notified the public that credit cards could no longer be used because their magnetized numbers failed to register. And toy magnets h ad become so strong that if toddlers swallowed them their hearts ceased beating. Industrial production had declined because magnets were vital to factories. A world-wide recession would result.

Photographs from the International Space Station showed tiny yellow rings, faint and almost translucent, forming at both poles, moving slowly.

"Is the swap inevitable?" Dahlia said, anxious now.

"Perhaps," Darius answered., "A rereversal could occur."

"Why?"

"If likes repel, they might prove too similar and return to their original places."

"But they're from the opposite ends - -"

"Yes. The antipodes."

"- - and might attract. In which case we're doomed." Wendy said.

To barbarism or extinction like the dinos, Darius thought. Unless - -

Walter was staring through the window. "Dark clouds, lightning."

"So?" Darius asked.

Walter squinted. "Not just ordinary lightning - -ball lightning, the most destructive."

"How do you know?"

"I'm an e.e., remember?"

A jet engine roared in the sky but the group was watching a ball of flame ignite a tree.

"I need a better view," Walter shouted and rushed to the roof.

Darius went with him and said, "This is too hazardous." He headed back downstairs. The phone rang but he hadn't time to answer.

"The house might catch fire," Wendy shrieked and also retreated.

They reached the cellar where the Aleuts lurked.

"We've fireproofed the basement," Joe told them.

"It's safe here," Josie said. "More tests?"

"No time for them," Darius said. "I have to check the Intermagnet."

To escape the Aleuts and their demand for tests, he climbed to the kitchen where the group assembled. Alfonso Jackson reported, "The golden (not yellow) rings have increased their velocity to perhaps twenty miles per hour, a speed that will give us decades to adjust or discover solutions."

"A techno-optimist," Darius raged. "And probably wrong."

"No," Walter argued. "Probably correct."

"That mirrors your right-wing political position," Darius countered. "Conservative."

"Is there a liberal answer?"

"We must change."

A parachute dropped near the tree and a man stood up, removing his goggles. He was short with a high forehead and small, wideset eyes which seemed to glare. "I know who you are." He said.

"How?" Darius demanded.

"I've been monitoring your communications ever since you heard from Alfonso Jones, the fool."

"Fool. Why?"

"A Negro Jew? Disgusting! But that's not the reason I came."

"What is?"

"I urge you to leave right away. I'll take you on my jet seaplane, parked near the beach. We'll fly to Sweden where I live."

Darius snapped his fingers. "You must be Alfred Nobel."

"Right. But I don't manufacture explosives. I'm a scientist."

"You can afford a jet seaplane?"

"That carries extra large fuel tanks. But that's not how I earn my fortunes. I invest in credit default insurance companies. As the geomagnetic polar reversal approaches, panic will ensue and businesses collapse. I'll teach you the method of making a fortune."

"What will you do with yours?"

"Die happy."

"No," Wendy said. "We're trying to figure out a means of surviving a polar upside down."

"Rots of ruck," Nobel's accent has emerged, Darius thought. "I must hurry before the tide goes out. Take me to the beach."

"O.K.," Dahlia grumbled. "But I need a reward."

All of them Humveed to the beach. His parachute providing flotation, Nobel paddled to the enormous plane. Women in uniforms hoisted him on board and the aircraft took off.

Dahlia found a baby seal trying to swim in the surf and scooped it into her arms. "About the same size as Taca," she remarked. "I'll name her Raca for Resolute."

Something flashed in the distance and they heard an explosion. "Ball lightning," Walter surmised. "At least he died happy."

"Hmmm," Darius mouthed. "I wonder what the radio says."

Walter switched on the short-wave radio and they listened. Static, then." Nome, Alaska, here. I need to talk with someone. Loud noises in my head and they're getting really bad. I've tried to call the hospital but the phone is out. Won't somebody hear me? I'm a widower and alone. WOLF."

"A lone wolf," Wendy joked.

"No laughing matter," Darius said. "Nome isn't that far away. I wonder what Magsat has to tell us."

Intermagnet gave the latest reading. A golden ring, miles wide, had formed over Alaska.

"The ralop paws," he began.

Dahlia, looking alarmed, scurried to the basement. "Earth thirty-nine," she said.

He looked at the computer. "The rings are expanding. They cover the horizon from coast to coast and, now, the oceans, Eurasia, Africa, South America, Australia and Antarctica. The rings are now universal. The info must have come from Magsat."

Wendy asked, "What about the rings' effect, Walter?"

He activated the radio, reaching area after area in the U.S.

Chapter Nine

EARTH THIRTY-SIX

WHAT IS MAXIMUM? DARIUS asked himself and said, after consulting the Intermagnet, "Earth forty. Not long now. Walter, how does the compass read?"

He went to the roof, returned and said, "Heading south."

"Oh dear," Dahlia muttered. "I confess I'm worried." She held up the baby seal and inspected its belly. "Is little Raca hungry?"

"Your darling pet must eat fish," Wendy said.

"No fish," Dahlia answered. "He…she…has to be thirsty."

"Its gender?" Wendy said.

"I don't know. All I see is flippers."

"Use your hand," Walter suggested.

"I don't want to. I'll give it some water."

She placed the infant seal on the floor and put a cup of water from the kitchen sink beside it. The seal lapped the whole cup.

Darius watched and fantasized. A baby dino became his loving pet. He'd name the creature Dino and feed it steak tartar, Dino would follow him wherever he went, wagging its tail and panting. It might step on his toe and he'd have to exercise caution. Dino would have to be housebroken. Thank God it couldn't fly!

The seal lay on its side and Dahlia wept. "What killed Raca?"

"The seal must be magnetized," Darius said. "All of us should drink only bottled water."

"Sey," Dahlia said.

"This is - -"

Place after place, each different in different fashions, one worse than the next. As time passed, it seemed clear the nation was falling into idiocy.

So many people used Backspeak as it was officially called now that communication turned impossible. Sign language was employed.

Double Backspeak meant talking in reverse in foreign tongues.

Cities like Los Angeles had demonstration before a Donald-Mac urging that glishEng become the official language.

Crime increased tenfold and so did traffic accidents since drivers, having lost their sense of direction, went the wrong way down one-way streets.

ʻNew road maps confused north and south - - Minneapolis lay south of St. Paul, they read. And if you aimed for Canada, you were directed to Mexico.

Microhard developed a software program that converted Backspeak into normal language.

During parades, the crowd marched backward, faces toward the rear. Confessed liars found themselves elected to public office.

People getting lost turned into a national problem. They roamed the countryside like buffalo herds. Relatives thought they should wear collars as do dogs. PETA organizations formed to protect humans.

"All?"

"Americans. Our civilization is, like the compass needle, going south."

"Toward?"

"Illiteracy. Chaos."

"More than other cultures?"

"Uh-huh. We're already verging on disaster."

"The same in the southern hemisphere?"

"I don't know. Perhaps the southern nations…Brazil, Ecuador, Argentina, the African ones…will inherit our energy and drive, though I believe they'll also be negatively affected by the ralop paws… Excuse me. Polar swap. What's happening in the Command Center's opinion?"

She read, "- - according to the President, America has never been stronger. Ours is the land of opportunity and free enterprise. To God we owe the precious gift of liberty and peace."

American jihad favored a new dark age.

"Down with the poor!" they chanted at rallies.

That the rich ruled was taken for granted.

"Kcuf" became a brand of clothes.

Health care plans were spurned despite the rapidly rising rate of skin cancer, blindness, and death.

On TV the public preferred commercials.

Democracy was replaced by pubocracy since people imbibed so much. Cigarette smoking increased to the point that tobacco and liquor levies substituted for income taxes.

The American flag became a banner that read U.S. Army. The draft was reinstated.

Other countries must convert to Jesusianity or risk being atom-bombed.

"In God we trust" was sung at the national anthem.

Restaurants served only pizza, pasta and ice cream. The average American weighed three hundred pounds, the women a little more than the men.

Attorney generals of the U.S. no longer required a law degree. All top officials had to be called generals - - for instance the President general.

Only martial music played on T.V.

Air Force One was now a stealth bomber.

The cost of flying the President, Vice President and their staffs exceeded the budget of many countries.

A toothpaste was named Presodent. Only dentists bought it.

A new brand of car, the Magnobile, automatically sounded its horn when pedestrians appeared.

A million pounds of beef were recalled because the cattle received human conditions.

That was how Darius envisioned the future.

"A ballscrew society," he concluded.

#

"We'll watch VT," Dahlia ordered.

"Ballscrew? VT?" Wendy questioned.

Darius and Dahlia swapped glances. They seemed ashamed but she went calmly to the livingroom.

Click.

Announcer: "Things have been growing here in L.A. and not just fear. We've already reported - -"

"We haven't been watching," Wendy said.

" - - the rapid plant growth. The hills behind Malibu now have a canopy of vegetation like a Brazilian rain forest. Scientists at UCLA's biomagnetic lab which specializes in hydrology believe our water is magnetized. Research, they claim, has shown magnetized H^2O causes plants to expand their roots and leaves, hence luxuriant foliage. And it's happened in a matter of days.

"Flower stores claim only magnolias are selling."

"More gradual has been the appearance of a new breed of healer. Magnotherapist fans say the practitioners are surrounded by an aurora and their touch restores health by clearing clogged arteries and gallstones. They increase neurohormones, chemical compounds that absorb excess magnetism, although they admit they don't understand what magnetism is. Still, the healers claim they imbue water with subtle magnetic life force."

"Meaning?" Dahlia asked.

"An energy field, I guess."

"Other news: in southern California wild animals are running everywhere as if they've lost their sense of direction, filling the roads. Dogs, cats, deer, skunks, opossums, cougars from the mountains. Nocturnal animals threaten to replace people in the cities. The roads are without cars which have ceased to work. Engines have been magnetized. (Images of stopped cars and frustrated drives,) Panic ensued, (Images of police with bullhorns.) Travel has come to a halt here. The economy - -, the economy - -"

"Why does he always expect himself?" Dahlia asked.

"The blood in his tongue must have magnetized," Wendy said. "It could happen to us."

"We're safer now," Darius observed.

"But how long?" Wendy said.

"Eternity," Walter insisted.

Darius wished he were a bio-scientist, instead of a physics one, because he'd be better able to predict the future.

They were interrupted by knocking on the door. An oiler rasped, "We've continued to drill. Always want more oil. But we've struck something funny."

"Funny ha-ha?" Dahlia said with a smile. The oiler frowned. "He must mean peculiar."

The man showed them a hunk of rock. Darius identified it, "Gabbros."

"What's peculiar about that?" Dahlia asked.

The man held up the rock which sparkled and glowed. "Nothing but electricity could have caused such a thing," Walter said. "Might the drill have short-circuited?"

"No. The camera could, however," the oiler said.

Darius stared at the rock, "I see tiny holes."

The rock crackled.

"It must have contained water which evaporated," Wendy diagnosed.

"And the rocks must become instant semiconductors," Walter marveled.

"Hypermagnetism could have caused the phenomenon," Darius explained. "Watch what the camera recorded?"

"Had to...the oil...reached a sub - -"

"Terranian - -"

"He must mean cave."

"The drill dropped."

"How deep?"

"Don't know. Very, through the camera, glimpsed a fiery ball. The mag - -"

"Magnometer."

"Went crazy."

The oiler departed.

Darius said, "I think he saw the outer edge of the earth's core which must be accelerating. Evidently, a polar reversal is near."

"We shouldn't be alarmed," Walter assured them. He turned on the radio, they listened and watched at the same time.

"California, the world's seventh largest economy, has declined. People feel too weak to function - -"

"I already told you the hemoglobin in one's blood can be magnetized," Wendy said. "I lived in a small town near Quebec. Lightning might destroy us. I blame a magnetic storm which knocked out Quebec many years ago. It could happen again."

"I'm in Kansas. We can't sell nolethan...excuse me, ethanol... because pumps all over the nation where cars still run, give faulty readings."

"In San Diego, firefighters aren't able to put out blazes since water gets stuck in the hoses."

"Magnetized water," Darius commented.

"I'm an ichthyologist - -"

"What's that?" Dahlia said again.

"He studies marine life," Darius answered.

"- - and the narwals are heading north into shark-infested water where they'll be doomed."

"Like us?" Wendy remarked and struggled to smile.

The group watched, "Yellow fog fills San Francisco. Yellow dogs have become invisible even to those with normal eyesight."

And they listened. "Hello there. I'm in the outback of Australia and our main occupation is eating. We netted a Narwhal, tagged as swimming from Baffin Island, and we'll have whale meat for supper. Mmmm, mmmm, good."

"He, at least, is happy," Dahlia remarked.

"Aren't you?" Walter asked.

"No. Too scared."

Again they watched. "Film writers, having struck for lower pay (images of picket lines) because their product is inferior, have failed and moved to China where they'll paint magnetic toys."

"Multiple opposites," Darius deduced. "As we've experienced under hypermagnetism. They must presage a polar flip-flop."

The group heard: "I'm from the District of Columbia. I'm sick of our candidates flip-flopping positions on the polar reversal. Either it's happening or it's not."

Darius looked at the computer. "I wonder what the Command Center has to offer."

FOUR

Chapter Ten

H E READ ALOUD, "ORGANIZED society has ceased to exist. Schools and factories are closed as well as offices. FEMA's arm, FEMMA, the Federal Magnetic Management Agency, has declared a state of emergency. Hospitals are open but only on a limited basis. Firefighters remain vigilant against arson and the police will prevent looting.

"Golden rings have been spotted in the ionosphere - -"

"Too far away to cause a catastrophe," Walter said.

"Wait," Darius warned.

"You said that before."

"- - and Magsat reports the van Allen belts are being compromised."

"See?" Darius muttered.

"You exhibit the I-told-you-so syndrome," Wendy observed.

Darius shrugged. "Que sera sera."

"Isn't that fatalistic?"

"Expect the best but prepare for the worst is my opinion and I don't mean liverwurst."

Wendy giggled.

"It isn't a joking matter. Check the compass, Gertz."

"O.K., Darius."

As Walter went upstairs, Dahlia asked, "Why the last name?"

"Perhaps formality indicates desperation."

They sat in silence.

Walter soon returned. "The needle points almost due south."

"As I said, prepare for the worst."

"How?" Wendy said.

"I wish I knew."

"Perhaps the Aleuts can help."

"Where are they?"

"In the basement, I think."

The group descended. The Aleuts sat in the module.

"What's happening?" Josie said to Darius.

"Everything and nothing."

"I don't understand."

"We're expecting something to happen that perhaps won't."

"You're speaking in circles," Joe said.

"The circles of hell," Walter added.

"Yes, it might be bad," Darius admitted. "We must take defensive measures."

"We're safe here," Josie said.

"Haven't you gained weight?" Darius said.

"Maybe a little."

"What measures?" Wendy questioned.

"We could flee," was Dahlia's idea.

"Escape is futile," Darius responded. "We can only try to remain sane."

"But shall we?"

Darius winced. He looked at Josie again.

#

That night it rained magnets - - the water was magnetized Darius discovered, using the magnometer he'd borrowed from the oil guys who'd departed because their equipment was stuck together.

"Rain gets into the well," Dahlia said. "We'll be magnetized."

"Nonsense," Walter scoffed and drank water laced with copious bourbon. Intoxicated, he staggered to the yard where he, now found, was covered with ferrous trash left by the former owners.

"At least I didn't attract cans," he said ruefully, removing carpenter nails and other steel pieces.

And he seemed to change. His right and left arms hooked together. His head bent toward his toes. "I've become the magnetic man."

"Unappealing," Wendy said and he returned to his former self.

"Was that a bi-polar episode?"

"I think so," Wendy said.

"Women, thank God, aren't composed of steel," Dahlia said and blushed.

"Perhaps they ought to be. I favor strong women."

"Such as I?" Wendy purred.

"I consider you as weak compared to me."

Darius saw

Walter + Wendy

But not

Dahlia + Darius

He wished he could but how?

Wandering into the yard, Darius found himself packed in soup cans. Why? Then he remembered that, if the magnetic field were superstrong, even tin would be magnetized.

I must resemble a pile of junk with tin cans and scrap metal hanging from me. I must seem ridiculous.

Goats appeared, gobbling the garbage and excreting garbage cans. "They seem invulnerable. If only we could copy them," Darius thought.

Back in the house, Dahlia frowned and said, "The trash man! I should feel sorry for you but I don't."

Dahlia + Darius

She added, "However, I remain fond of you."

Darius – Dahlia

Likes repel. Anti-positive magnetism. Was that the way to stay sane? And save the world?

EARTH FORTY

Darius returned to the basement and found Joe and Josie. "Where have you been?"

"Waiting for you," Joe declared from the insulated control booth.

Perhaps they'd be the last survivors, an Aleut Adam and Eve who'd repopulate the world. But, emerging, they might succumb to skin cancer and starvation because of blindness under a hostile sun like everybody else.

Darius saw in his mind's eye cities and towns under martial law as evacuation became compulsory. Graveyards filled the farmlands until space ran out. Perhaps, of course, that was just a dreadful fantasy.

He rushed upstairs and got Intermagnet on the computer. It told him the golden rings in the sky were descending and threatened to cross.

"The world will be flipped on its back," he said. "We won't know up from down."

"And our brain hemispheres will reverse," Wendy again warned.

"With - -"

Dahlia attempted to lighten things. "We'd turn topsy-turvy."

Silence.

"- - dire consequences," Wendy finished.

Walter had wired the compass so that where the needle pointed could be observed on the computer. "Almost due south," he shouted.

"Soon, the reversal will be complete," Darius said.

"No!" Wendy screamed. "I'm frightened."

Walter's tone was soothing. "Don't be. The swap will never happen."

"Why not?"

"Causebe - -" Walter looked askance and shut up.

"Because, he means," Wendy said.

"Because what?" Darius demanded.

Walter rechecked the computer and said, "Right all. I'm a vertcon." He shed tears.

"Next, he'll want a sex change," Dahlia grumbled.

They'd be permanent opposites, Darius thought and saw

$$Dahlia + Walter$$

which failed to please him. But if Wendy became a man

$$Walter + Wendy$$

However, that implied

$$Darius + Dahlia \text{ and/or } Wendy = 0$$

unless he switched genders too but he'd refuse. How about

$$Darius + Josie$$

She was saying, "The final test."

"Why final?"

"Because we quit," Joe said.

"But have you any last words?"

Wendy said. "I'll pay my parents what I stole."

Darius: "I'll never be cruel again to animals."

Walter: "I will pray at my brother Sol's grave."

Dahlia (sobbing): "I shouldn't have killed my father."

"O.K." said Josie and they disappeared.

"Where would they go?" Wendy wondered.

"To the tavern fast, I expect. Needed pleasure," Darius said. "So do we."

Without another word, he seized Dahlia's hand and dragged the woman upstairs to her bedroom. He'd never seen it before. A double bed lay before the casement window, offering a splendid view of green hills and the fields filled with wheat. Harvest time! Except who would be alive to pick the grain or eat it? No matter. Right now he had to know what sex with Dahlia would be like. Would she warm to him? And he her?

Thus far Dahlia hadn't resisted, perhaps swept away in a momentary thrill. Above all, he mustn't seem clumsy, groping. Love, not sex, should appear his objective. And her? The same, he hoped.

Eyes glazed, she dropped on the bed. Was it passive resistance or being coy? And how could he learn? Boldness was the answer so he tried to plant a kiss. Dahlia, thank God, returned the smooch but giggled.

Dahlia, he judged, was too juvenile for him, a high school cheerleader, as she'd said, trapped in time. He wanted an adult. Wendy?

He found her in the hall, waiting. For? It had to be him. Unsmiling, she led him upstairs and into her bedroom with lace curtains and a single bed just like his. He grasped instinctively they understood each other as she removed her coveralls and sat on the bed. He joined her and whispered "I love you", meaning it. They heard Walter's chuckles from Dahlia's room and then Darius and Wendy had marvelous sex.

He saw the absolute and final truth

Wendy + Darius

\#

Afterward, the group decided to visit the tavern on what might be their last night alive.

The Humvee refused to start…Walter believed the vehicle had been magnetized…and they walked.

The night was dark and gloomy with thick clouds obscuring the horizon. "We won't be able to see the northern ring," Darius said, "To accomplish that, we must return to the house and look at the computer."

"But first the tavern, I intend to get loaded," Walter announced.

I recall summer nights in Pasadena when you could see the stars and a warm breeze blew. In those days I was filled with hope - - anything seemed possible. Maybe I'd become a full professor and even the head of the department of paleomagnetism at Caltech. I had high hopes as in the song. Not now. My aspirations have dwindled to a single one - - survival of the human race. Can we? Can I? If so, I'll settle for Wendy and kids, middle-class ambitions. That's me - - middle-class. Proud of it. Will there be a class structure in the future assuming we survive? Or shall humans find themselves reduced to rabble? Another possibility: we evolve into a higher form, a dim prospect.

They reached the tavern where the sign read NNE. Inside the crowd clapped.

"The reason?" Dahlia asked the sloe-eyed waitress.

"Those folks think the compass needle will bring good luck to our village."

"Why?"

"Pointing almost north has never happened to us before. The same with good luck."

Predictably, Walter ordered a double bourbon on the rocks, Dahlia what passed for champagne, Wendy a gimlet, Darius nothing.

"I find no cause to celebrate," he said, and said it again, louder.

At the bar, the Eskimos booed.

"I'm just guessing, but bad luck must be construed as beneficial," Darius observed. "They must see things in reverse. It that a symptom of the polar event?"

A rhetorical question and nobody bothered to answer.

Joe rushed in from the dock, "I heard the spouting of whales. Probably belugas. They never come this far south. We'll harpoon them tomorrow."

"Tomorrow?" thought Darius. Will tomorrow for humans arrive?

Through the swinging doors Jeremy appeared. He whispered, "Praise be to dog - -"

"God, he means," Wendy translated.

"Who barks."

Then the preacher stood on his head.

Josie murmured, "Barking dog is great."

Walter glanced at the ceiling, "The electric fans spin in reverse."

"How are they supposed to spin?" Dahlia asked.

"Counter clock-wise, I believe."

"That's right to left?'

"I'm no longer sure."

"What are you talking about?"

Walter descended into deeper confusion. "Was it politics? I hope so. I lean clock-wise."

"That's left to right?"

"Perhaps."

"I give up."

The group, getting drunk (even Darius who imbibed the strong Eskimo beer) needed help so even Joe and Josie offered to shepherd them home.

"Which direction is it?" Dahlia mumbled.

Walter pointed.

"Wrong," Wendy claimed.

"No. That way," Dahlia said.

"You're all mistaken," Darius muttered.

The Aleuts plodded down the straight road, the group behind. Lightning flashed, making it seem like instant daylight. "Weird," Dahlia marveled.

"Ball lightning," the e.e. reminded. "Rare but not impossible."

"We're almost home," Josie said. "Come to our house."

The group followed Joe and Josie to an igloo shaped cement structure behind the graveyard.

"The nearest we can get to how our ancestors lived," Joe said.

Inside the pseudo-igloo the group was forced to stoop, even Wendy. "I'm claustrophobic," she admitted and they went to the graveyard, mist trailing them.

"Ghosts," Dahlia whispered, trembling.

"Impossible but rare," Darius said illogically.

They were sober upon reaching the house which creaked in the gale-force wind.

"Will it collapse?" Dahlia asked.

The Aleuts shrugged.

"Where would we go?" Wendy said. "Home?"

"I doubt it," Darius answered.

"Right," Walter said. "The planes - -'"

In the livingroom, Dahlia switched on the TV which still functioned.

Announcer: "L.A. is being evacuated. Traffic has come to a halt (Images long lines of vehicles.) LAX has completely shut down. No word on when the airport will resume flights. A reason, many pilots insist their vision has been impaired - -"

"UV radiation," Darius explained.

"- - the same holds true throughout the world. In Pakistan, the President has declared martial law after pilots went on strike, declaring aircraft no longer safe - -"

"Martial law could happen here," Darius predicted.

"- -and people say they've seen UFO's - -"

Click.

Having pressed the remote, Dahlia said, "Incredible. UFO's don't exist."

"What they really witnessed was the outer fringe of the northern ring."

"How fast does it travel?"

"Slow but the circumference is huge."

"It should be close."

"Perhaps above us."

The Aleuts stayed but the group rushed outside, gasping as they spotted the apparition.

The ring seemed translucent, a golden web against a black sky, trailing filaments like a giant jellyfish wrapping around world, sliding down until meeting its antithesis, the southern ring. For a moment, they would combine into a single ring and then the marriage would end, with each ring proceeding to the opposite pole from which they'd started.

Darius, who'd imagined this, realized he'd mixed metaphors. But the danger was real.

The group returned to the house where Darius discussed the phenomenon. "It's safe to say no one understands the thing. How could it be like that? A blind alley. Nobody knows. We can only theorize." He raised his hands in despair.

The basement computer still worked and Darius checked the Washington Command Center. An anti-magnetism shelter had been devised and the President, his cabinet, the Supreme Court, the Congress and their various staffs had taken refuge there. The Vice President remained in the White House in case the magnetism-proof shelter failed and the President perished, although the Veep expected to die first. The military was on full alert but the commanders feared cruise missiles meant to destroy the rings couldn't be properly aimed.

"Will we lose our lives?" Dahlia said tremulously.

"Of course," Wendy said, and once more explained how vital organs must fail because red blood cells would be magnetized. "You couldn't move."

"Show us," Walter said.

The portable MRI perched in a corner. It was four feet tall and about two feet wide. "Stick you leg in," she ordered.

Walter obeyed. To the MRI was attached a visiplate demonstrated the results: his circulation had almost completely halted.

"How does the leg feel?"

"Sort of numb."

"You're dying," Wendy said.

Walter giggled.

Darius frowned and rechecked the Intermagnet. It showed pictures of outer space from the modernized Hubble Telescope. What am I seeing? Is it reality or my imagination? Space seemed to unfurl as if on an endless treadmill. Stars, the Milky Way, then other galaxies, millions, no billions of galaxies, each containing tens of millions or even billions of stars, and their grouping in clusters and upper clusters of galaxies: the distant evidence of stars being born and dying; such star-like entities as quasars, each apparently producing more than 100 times the energy radiated by the billions of stars in the Milky Way, and pulsars, one which as recently found to rotate 640 times in one second; the invisible halos of galaxies, each contains as much as 90% of the galactic mass; string-like structures more than a hundred light years long and a light year wide, cutting across the central region of our galaxy; the "bubbles" in space, extending millions of light years, seemingly devoid of stars; intergalactic and interstellar matter, including a variety of organic molecules; apparent planets outside the Milky Way; "black holes" from which light can't escape; and the universe's background radiation. Thought to be the remnants of the very first moments of creation.

He thought he saw more. The treadmill rolled into infinity. How far back did it go? Or forward? Was there a limit to human knowledge? Were things intelligible or forever beyond our grasp?

Even the question was almost impossible to frame because it implied we'd never comprehend the endless universe. What did that mean? He couldn't hazard a guess.

And a hundred or a thousand years from now? The answer would be the same were his suppositions correct.

He attempted to explain it. "Above all feeling lonely in an incomprehensible universe - - ," but Walter had been listening to the radio, volume turned up when Darius ceased speaking.

"- - I've been hearing from hams all over America and I know for a fact that people are getting lost, complaining their muscles were sore - -"

As must happen everywhere, I think. We can watch the end of the world before the electricity stops. Such a thing has never happened before. Ball lightning will destroy the power lines. Place by place, darkness will descent. Civilization in its death throes. We have to remain inside. Danger lurks outdoors.

Josie screeched, "Got to go. Need fresh air." Joe followed her upstairs.

"Claustrophobic," Wendy judged.

Walter limped to the roof and returned.

"What happened?"

"I can't walk. My legs hurt."

"I warned you."

"But I'm not dead yet."

"Still not able to climb stairs."

Walter dragged himself up, using the railing.

The others followed. "I'll get a wheelchair," Dahlia said and pulled one from a closet. "Thank the former owners."

Walter wheeled to the kitchen. "I haven't told you what I saw?"

Prodded, he revealed ball lightning had reduced the Aleuts to sizzling strips of fat.

Darius almost retched but started the computer. Intermagnet appeared on the screen with images from Magsat which showed the golden rings approaching each other.

Not much time and so much to be resolved. Will humans (including us) survive? In hell or happiness? The latter, I hope.

The rings drew closer.

Whom will I end with?

Darius + Wendy

Romance vs. common sense. I tend to be practical, Wendy! But it might also depend on

Dahlia + Walter

Will she love him?

None of this will matter if we die and how would we? A number of ways are possible. The house is struck by ball lightning he heard the noise of falling bricks and the chimney must have collapsed and we perish in flames; hypermagnetism drives us crazy and we commit suicide. Or we kill each other. Who first?

Darius rushed to the basement. The rings on the screen seemed to have slowed. Why? Likes repel? But opposites attract and polar swaps have happened many times in the past. A reason for hope?

He envisioned a baby dino at his side and threw it a ball. Dino retrieved it, smiled and showed teeth. Darius parted the thick hide and bit his arm. No reason for hope.

But he heard a gurgling from the module. In it he saw an infant with oblong eyes. Josie's! She'd been obese and he realized she'd been pregnant. Would the baby survive? He wondered as the light blinked and the screen faded. The dim sign read

EARTH FORTY-ONE

The infant whimpered.